# The Cursed Fae
## The Power That Saves
### Book 2

1

# Contents

# CHAPTER 1

It has been three years since I've started school, I'm a Junior in college and I still don't have my powers that were supposed to manifest when I turned eighteen. On top of that my sister thinks my partying is out of control.

I thought the hardest thing about turning eighteen outside of trying to figure out what to wear to prom, was trying to figure out if my power was going to show up on my birthday. It had been the worst birthday ever seeing my sister get her powers but nothing good happening to me.

Those three months were frustrating, to say the least. Everyone had been so wrapped up with trying to figure out why Rosie had such a weird power that no one had even taken real notice that I Rosalyn HAD NO POWERS! It sucked. I mean sucked. Rosie gets this really cool power and she doesn't even want it, while I'm over here wishing I had any power.

Shoot, she could transfer her power to me then everyone would be happy. Well, at least I would be happy. I'm the oldest, I should have gotten the powers first, I was born first. Man, this is so unfair. My sister didn't understand what I was going through, she felt as if I was overreacting.

"Are you even listening to me?"

"What?" I asked beginning to get frustrated with this entire situation.

"I asked are you sure you're not still upset that I have a power and you don't? I mean you've been partying a lot."

"Of course, I meant it, not only do I love you, you're my baby sister and my twin. This is not a competition. Also, I party because I'm a human at college doing human things."

3

"But you're not human. You're still Fae with some form of powers that could be exploited and found out if you're not careful."

"Those powers are the basics and there is no reason they could bring our kind into the light. So if you don't mind can you kindly back off, if you love me then you would allow me to enjoy the life that I have been dealt. I'm headed out anyway."

When I woke the next morning I was still a dud. I didn't' have a new power and I probably never will.   I feel defective and trying to keep this from my sister is becoming harder and harder.

We have always been close, yet I don't feel as if I can talk to her about this. She has her own problems with this new power and the fact that it's not working the way it should. My parents not only can't explain it to her. they have no way of telling her how to work it. All they can think to say is, try to find the feeling you were feeling when it happened the first time.

What is the point of even going into nursing if I don't have the one power I want, to do the job I want, better than I would be able to do it?  Without the power, I'm a dud, defective, more human than Fae, a throwback. And I have no one to talk about this with.  I refuse to talk to Danielle. I know what she would say.

Ros, you are overreacting, your powers will come in, you are not a dud, and you could never be defective. How do I know this? Because she has already said it to me just last month. And yet I'm still sitting here on the way to the beginning of my life with not a power to my name.

Okay, I know I need to stop feeling sorry for myself. There is nothing wrong with being human. I mean my bestfriend is human and she is the best. I know a lot of great humans. So what, I won't be able to touch a person and heal them.

I'll still study as hard as I can and do what I can do when I can do it. Instead of Pediatrics, I'll just go into hospice, since they are dying anyway, I can be the human with the big heart to make them as comfortable as possible in the end.

With that figured out. I've decided to have the best college experience ever. Which means enjoying this party tonight.

⊕

I'm back from the best party I have been to since being here, I was feeling good up until Rosie came in my room to talk to me once again about going out and not studying as much as she thinks I should be doing. She must have seen the look on my face because she sat on the bed and grabbed my hands to beseech me her great wisdom.

She told me that if I stop worrying about it, my power might manifest, that soon it will happen. I'm the cause according to her. I know she means well, and if I thought about it deep down, I know she's right, it's still frustrating though.

What else is there for me to do but to listen to my sister, my twin, she would never tell me anything bad or wrong. The best thing for me is to listen to her advice. Rosie proceeds to tell me that one day I'll have power and I'll be able to prove myself great.

Who does she think she is, it's easy for her to say that when she has powers. One piece of advice I'm going to take from her is to look on the bright side. It's better not having powers that way I can party all I want when I want.

I knew I would love being away from home for the first time, and I would love my school learning new things and spending valuable time with my friends. And for the most part, it is. If I can just get my sister to leave me alone then it will be perfecto.

5

At the end of my Sophomore year, 1 met a cool guy named Kenneth James, but everyone calls him KJ except for me. When we first met we had a good time together. We partied, hung out, went to the park, just kicked it whenever we could.

He's cool peeps and we got along. A girl couldn't ask for more. So when he hit me up at the beginning of this year wanting to hang out 1 thought it would be the perfect distraction to my life.

No one understands or gets why it bothers me so much that 1 don't have powers, they look at me with pity. But 1 don't need their pity when I'll have parties. 1 have a high metabolism, so drinking doesn't bother me, and regardless of what they may think 1 would never use hard drugs even though there are several others at the parties that do.

That's the reason my family and friends think my relationship with him is toxic because he sells Medical Marijuana. 1 mean come on its 2019 everyone is smoking Marijuana. As long as I'm not doing it 1 feel they should mind their own business. When Rosie finds out we are back hanging again this year, she might just blow a gasket.

Since 1 have classes tomorrow, she doesn't have to worry about tonight, but I'll be going out with my human friends this weekend so she can cool her jets on thinking she can tell me what to do. As long as my grades stay up to par then there is nothing my parents would say, and she knows that. Another reason 1 will continue to party is, 1 know what I'm doing is not hurting anyone, especially myself.

1 woke the next morning feeling drained and not myself. 1 know that 1 have not had the energy I'm used to. Maybe I'm losing even the weak Fae powers 1 was born with since my others didn't manifest.

With my luck, it wouldn't surprise me if that was true. Thinking back I can't remember the last time I was up to going to the gym or for a run. Maybe that's what I need to do. Get back into my running.

Maybe Rosie is right, if I party less and think more of the physical, things would change for me. I'll think about it but not this weekend, this weekend is the first back to school party being held at Zelta Dolta. Of course, I can't invite the crew.

I could hear them now, why are you going there Ros, don't you remember what they did in Freshman year. Blah Blah Blah. I can live without it. I'll just go with Kenneth and his crew as usual.

After getting dressed for class leaving my room, I think I chose the wrong moment to come out. "So Rosalyn any plans this weekend?" asked Danielle. They were all standing there looking at me. They must have been waiting to ambush me as soon as I came out of the room. "Why does it matter what I'm doing this weekend?"

Rosie putting her fist on her hips. "Don't get offensive, we wanted to know because the crew is going camping this weekend before it gets too cold and we wanted you to join us since you haven't hung out with us in such a long time." Why is she bringing up last year? School just started and she already complaining about me hanging with them.

"Oh well, you all should have given me a heads up, I have plans with my guy this weekend, maybe another time. Anyway, I got to get to class." Who do they think they are to spring that on me, go camping. Why would I want to go camping with them? They don't like Kenneth so it's not like I can invite him. Nope.

Everyone will probably have their boyfriend or girlfriend there like last time we went camping and I was there by myself with them constantly telling me not to feel like a fifth wheel, more like the seventeenth wheel. No thank you.

7

Matter of fact, after that camping trip, is when I met Kenneth I bumped into him as I was storming into the Sophomore building cursing myself for actually going on that trip. And we've been hanging ever since.

After class I was hoping when I got back to the room to change for the party no one would be there, I was in luck. Looking at the clock I had time to jump in the shower. I love taking showers in the junior building, they have something the freshman and sophomore building don't, one-way windows.

We can see out but no one can see in. I enjoy standing in the shower and looking at the view. Since it's raining outside you would think taking a shower is crazy. But it helps me to relax.

Standing in the shower, I start to think of the last two years and I can't help but wonder if maybe I have been doing things the wrong way, maybe I need to come to terms with my situation. So what my power didn't manifest. Yeah, who am I fooling, my lifelong dream was to heal sick babies.

Looking out the window it's ironic that it's raining as I'm standing here shedding tears I've been holding in for so long. Why did this happen to me? All I ever wanted to do with my life is to help heal sick babies. What good am I now? I'm useless.

I need this party more than anything. Shaking off the tension I wash up, step out the shower, and get the surprise of my life. As soon as I step out lightning strikes through the window. That was close, one more second and I would've been electrocuted. I guess my Mom saying never shower when it's raining was real.

That was so freaky, I have to make sure to tell the school. But if I do and they cement the windows everyone will hate me. I'll just spread the word and let everyone come to their own conclusion, let the majority decide. Right now I have to get ready for this party.

While dressing my phone dings. I hope it's not Rosie.

I'm downstairs.

Cool otw.

We walking so bring an umbrella.

I should have known that he wouldn't go for driving since the party is so close, plus it makes no sense, it's only a ten-minute walk. I realized that in the rain ten minutes seems longer and by the time we got here, I'm ready to party. It could have something to do with the flask that Kenneth had for us to keep us warm on the walk.

The party was going great, I was having a good time and of course, the smile on Kenneth face laughing it up with his guys showed me he was having a great time also. We always make sure to mingle and make rounds for about an hour before diving into the libations. "You want a drink? He asked me leaning over to whisper in my ear.

"Yeah a beer is good, I'm not doing the house punch anymore ever." He laughed at that.

Last year I did the house punch and off one cup I ended up face down in my bed until two days later. They said it was shifter strong, but that was going beyond a punch for shifters. Not happening again.

While waiting for my beer, an EMT crew came rushing into the party and heading outback. I ran that way to see what was going on. Looking around to see if I saw Kenneth I noticed that he was already out there. Sliding up beside him. "What's going on?"

He looks at me as if seeing me for the first time. "I don't know, I was on my way to bring you your drink when they passed so I followed them out." A guy was walking past crying, Kenneth grabbed his arm as he was headed inside. "Hey what's going on?"

"Doug overdosed. We don't know what he was on but whatever it was he overdosed." With that, he pulled his sleeve out of Kenneth's grip and walked into the house.

Kenneth grabbed my hand. "Come on Rosalyn we need to get out of here before the school security shows up or the police."

"Why? We don't have anything to do with this." I lowered my voice to a whisper. "Weed doesn't do that so you good."

"Not if they find it on me I'm not. You can stay. I'm out."

Of course, I wasn't going to let him leave without me. That's not what girlfriends do. "I'm coming." Walking home we were quiet. It was surreal that a kid would overdose here. I've never heard of it happening before on this campus. When we got back to the building he told me that he was going to head out, which meant I would be heading upstairs by myself with my thoughts.

No hanging out and watching late night tv down here in the common area with him. Being alone with my thoughts. That's a scary idea. Maybe I should grab my gear and go join everyone on their camping trip. Naw, they would just ask too many questions I don't want to answer.

# CHAPTER 2

When I got back to the room I laid across my bed the short way on my back. I don't know how long I laid there but I must have fallen asleep because the next thing I knew my phone was dinging with a text message from Rosie asking me if I wanted her to bring me something back from the store. They were on their way back. I had slept all night. it was midday on Sunday.

I guess I was more exhausted than I thought I was. After texting Rosie back that I was good, grabbing a shower, and going down to the lunchroom to grab a quick sandwich. I decided to head to the library to do some needed studying for a quiz I had to take this Monday.

While in the library I overheard some students talking about a party that was happening next weekend, but it was very exclusive and invitation only. Something about a high-level secret poker game being included and the last thing they needed was the police finding out.

I bet at that kind of party Kenneth could make a killing with his weeds sales. So, of course, being the best girlfriend that I am I sent him a text telling him what I had just heard and that if he can finagle an invite I was his plus one.

Who would pass up a chance to go to an all exclusive party? I can only imagine the high-end drinks that they will be serving, not that cheap stuff that is always served at the Frat parties. Keg beer, stale spiked punch, and cheap whiskey. Nope, this is going to be next level partying. Too bad I can't invite Rosie and the rest of them. They probably wouldn't approve anyway.

After studying and working a little on a report that was due next week I returned to the room to find it empty outside of Samantha. She looked at me and rolled her eyes. Something is seriously wrong with that chick. I went into my room and closed the door behind me.

I even locked it for good measure, not that I was scared of her, but if she chose to talk to me for any reason, my locked door would let her know she was not welcomed.

I didn't know and didn't care about what happened for the rest of the night. I do know that I was well-rested by time I came out of my room the next morning to head to the showers. "Good morning ladies," I called out coming out of my room. "I'm going to grab a quick shower then head down for some breakfast. Did you all want to join me?"
Rosie raised her eyebrow. "For breakfast, not the shower nerd. I think I can take a shower by myself."

Rosie laughed, "I know what you meant. I just like giving you a hard time." I stuck out my tongue and jogged out the room and down the hall to get ready for the day. It's becoming easier and easier to put on a brave face for my family and friends. The last thing I need is for them to get all up in my business.

We all went down to breakfast, when the guys showed up I assumed Rosie texted Augustas before I came back from the shower or they sniffed us out. While we were eating, the biggest surprise was when Kenneth joined us, even more, was the PDA.

We had a strict no PDA rule, that wasn't what our relationship was made of, but that did not stop him from picking me up out my seat, taking said seat and then placing me on his lap like it was the most natural thing to do. I played it off and continued to eat my food as if nothing happened.

12

After a few minutes, he leaned in and whispered in my ear. "We're in. This weekend, I received an invite without even really trying." I smiled even bigger. Oh yeah, this is going to be the best weekend ever.

I stood up after finishing off my bacon, "It was nice hanging with you guys, but I must get to class. Professor Ox is exactly that, a big fat OX shifter with the attitude to boot. If you're late you have to stand the entire class, he says only students that are on time deserve the pleasure of sitting."

"Isn't that against some kind of school rule?" Asked Marlo.

"Don't know and I don't care. Catch you all later." When I looked back at the table I noticed that Kenneth had not gotten up. What was he playing at? Getting close to my friends was also not a part of our deal. We had established where we were going and we both knew that I was not his mate, and so us being together past college was a no go.

Looks like I'm going to have to reiterate our deal. Fun only, No ties. I'm not putting my heart into a shifter when I know I'm not his true mate. Plain and simple, and if I was Kenneth true mate he would have told me by now.

After my classes, I texted Kenneth to see if he wanted to meet me at the ice cream shop in town. He said he couldn't since he had a meeting with Pent. I promise that man never has time during the week for me to see him. After texting Rosie to let her know where I was going I headed into town to get me a banana split with lots of whip cream and chocolate syrup.

I decided to walk so I could do a little thinking about Kenneth. Maybe it's time to part ways. If his feelings are getting deeper than I'm comfortable with. I should end it now instead of later. Come to think of it I do remember a few weeks ago him saying something about being able to be with someone who is not his true mate as long as they bind together. Dummy me, well he can

13

hang that up. No way am I soul binding myself to him or anyone else. No, nope, no way, not happening.

When I arrived at the shop I remembered why it was a bad thing to put ice cream in a text to my sister, if one thing she could never resist its ice cream. So I was not surprised when I came into the shop to find the girls and Augustas there sitting at a table. "How did you guys beat me here?"

Rosie pointed at me, "legs." Then she pointed at Augustas. "Car." Well, that said it all. I did enjoy spending time with them, and I hated having to hide things from them, and when we spent this fun time together I felt a tad bit guilty. If I knew they would understand I would share everything with them. But the last thing I need is the judgment from them about Kenneth's side job and me still being with him.

⊕

The rest of the week went by without incident and in a flash. I had to work even though I didn't manifest a power I still got my dream job of being a nurse and working with babies. The only thing that concerned me was the number of overdoses that were coming into the clinic.

I think this week we had maybe six. Two of them fatal. It's sad when young folks lose their life. It's even worse when someone is out there pushing this mess knowing it's killing people just to make a few dollars.

When Saturday came I was so giddy. I didn't know why exactly. I mean I've been to plenty of parties before. I guess since this was so exclusive I felt like some type of royalty, even though I didn't get the invite. Who would know? No one that's who. So I'm milking it for all it's worth.

When I got in the car I looked at Kenneth, he looked good in his dark washed jeans, a black Polo shirt, and a leather jacket. "Hey bae, do you know how to play poker?" I asked him.

14

"Yes, of course. I might not play though it depends on the stakes and the tables. I only brought like five with me."

"Well five hundred dollars is nothing to sneeze at. They shouldn't have tables higher than that should they?"

Kenneth laughed, "no my love, not five hundred, five thousand. I asked around, the reason these games are so exclusive is that they are high stakes. The buy-in is five hundred."

"What!, who in their right mind would risk losing that much money?"
"The same person in their right mind would risk winning that much money."

"I guess, I'll just mingle and drink. So I'm not bored."

"Sounds like a plan. I also heard they have a tv room that will be playing different games on several televisions as if you are in a sports bar."

"Whose place is this anyway?"

"Don't know. There is never a name on the invite, however, whoever It is they are extremely strict. They have security, and everyone is subject to being searched for weapons. It's not just shifters that are invited to these functions, and some people get upset when they lose a lot of money. Also, there is a buffet-style set up I heard so there will be food. Just enjoy yourself, babe, that's all I want. Okay?"

When we arrived the number of cars was ridiculous. Oh, whoever was throwing this little shindig was going to make a killing tonight. When we went inside there were levels to this place. The first floor was dancing, food, and a bar. Two sets of stairs led up to the second floor where there were double doors.

Inside the room were ten tables and chairs in the middle of the floor set up with dealers awaiting the start of the game. Next to this room was another door with a sign that said tv room. Inside was about five televisions attached to the wall, two bars with barstools, and a jukebox in the corner, with two-two-person high tables and chairs around.

After the guided tour. I started my night at the bar. "Hey, did you want to go into the tv room? Asked Kenneth. I also heard there is a game room downstairs in the basement with pool tables. If you wanted to go down we can run a game before the poker game starts up. I figured I would sit down for a few hands before mingling again."

"That sounds like a plan." I was not surprised to see that even downstairs there was a bar. This person was making money all over the place. The bars and poker tables weren't free but everything else was, even the jukebox all you had to do was pick a song.

"I need to throw one of these. I mean come on think of the money." I said.

"I hear you on that. He has to be very well known for so many people to be here. This is outstanding. I like the way this person rolls. Come on you rack them." Said, Kenneth.

Kenneth and I were never serious when it came to playing pool. We didn't take focused shots. We didn't aim we just hit the white ball and wherever it went it was good with us. The reason for this was the fact that I'm a pool shark. I have been playing pool since I was like ten with my big cousins so I'm exceptionally good at it, and Kenneth has also been playing so long that we realized unless we just have fun games our games would be long-lasting.

16

Now, I'm usually not the type of person to take another person's money, but when said person is obnoxious I don't care. I know that Kenneth can play pool and Kenneth knows I can play. Which means our game should be of no concern to anyone but us.

I guess when you are in a house full of gamblers that is not the case. A guy was standing at our table watching us play pool and decided that heckling us was the way to go. "You two suck at playing pool."

Kenneth looked at him and walked past to take another goofy shot. "You don't know what you're talking about." He took his shot and of course he missed. That was the point. To make our game fun and last longer.

When I went to the table to take my shot, again the guy had something to say, "the obvious shot would be the six ball, only an amateur would go for the shot you're trying to attempt." I looked at him. "That's the point, bug off and let us enjoy our game."

Looking at Kenneth. "I have two thousand dollars that say me and my lady can beat the pants off you and your lady."

Kenneth was about fed up by then, "look, buddy, why don't you go and find someone else to hassle. Me and my lady can actually play, we are making shots that won't go in on purpose, so scamper off. Okay."

He laughed, and I don't mean a subtle laugh, no you would think he was at a comedy show how hard he laughed. "You expect me to believe that? If that is true then put your money where your stick is."

I looked at Kenneth, "digging out some money from my purse. Here is my half. Come on babe, we need to put him in his place. If we make it quick we can get back to our game."

He kissed me, "you so get me."

The guy was so confident in his ability to beat us that he called over his buddies and had the audacity to put on side bets. "You guys can break first," I said, "because once we get on the table we won't be getting off." The rules of doubles are that each person takes three shots each until either there were no balls left on the table or one of you missed and the next team went.

"If you're sure?" Smart mouth commented with a smirk in his tone. I couldn't wait to wipe the floor with this guy.

Kenneth bobbed his head, "very."

His lady broke and she sunk one solid ball, her next two turns she sunk the balls she went for. When the guy came to the table, I could tell that this was going to go faster than I thought, not only did he not know how to play pool, he didn't even really know how to hold the pool stick. That is why he chose us, he figured he was a shoe in to win. Wrong move. He missed his second shot.

Kenneth and I flipped a coin to see who would go first, he won. Shoot, I wanted to be the person to send in the eight ball. But since Kenneth was going first he will shoot last if he doesn't miss, and like me, he doesn't. When we got on the table we never got off. We wiped the floor with them, and every shot we took I could see the guy getting madder and madder.

However, he was getting what he deserved. We tried to tell him we could play he just wouldn't listen. When Kenneth sunk the eight ball. I walked over to the money and as soon as I picked it up the guy grabbed my wrist.

"I don't think you two deserve to win since you thought it would be fun to hustle me."

I grabbed him by his balls with the hand he wasn't holding. "I would advise you to let me go before you lose more than your money. If you remember we asked you to leave us alone, we even told you we could play and the way we were playing was how we like to play each other. You wouldn't listen. So you got what you asked for."

Now, I know a person would be thinking at this moment why was I defending myself, where was Kenneth, he was being held back by a group of guys throwing out explicit of what was going to happen if he got loose. The lady was the smart one, she grabbed her guy's arm and pulled him away.

I did find out that his name was Harry. The group of guys didn't let Kenneth go until the couple had left the basement. Go figure that is when security showed up.

Kenneth walked up to me then, "are you alright? I'm going to kill that guy if I ever see him again."

"I'm fine, and please don't do manslaughter on my behalf it's not worth it. He didn't hurt me. I believe his balls are more injured than my wrist."

"No babe."

"Yes. Can we just enjoy the rest of our night? I'm having fun and I just came up a thousand bucks."

"If you're sure?"

"I Promise. Now can we get back to our game of goofy shots?"

"Yeah, come on. Your break." And that time we were able to enjoy our game without being harassed, haggled, or bothered at all.

19

Someone did come over and ask us what we were playing since he saw us play and knew we could. I explained the game and told him it was our way of not being competitive with each other, just having fun with playing pool.

Kenneth looked at his watch, "Hey Ros, the poker games are about to start. Did you want to go in the room with me?"

"Nope, I don't want to watch you play poker. I'm headed to the tv room. Come in there when you get done."

I was in the tv room for about an hour sitting at the bar when I overheard two guys near me talking about an underground fight club that one of them was involved in. Underground MMA fight club. I could do that. However it being underground meant secretive, how could I find it?

My question was answered when one of the guys stated that he had a fight that night and would be leaving soon. He just never passes up a chance to come to one of these. He would hate to not check-in and get eliminated from the guest list.

It's hard to get on and it's limited to only a hundred people. I'll have to make sure to tell Kenneth that little tidbit just in case he ever gets another invite and choose not to go. He should know the consequences.

But for now, I need to figure out how to get out of here and follow this guy to the fight and come back before Kenneth was done. Good thing I was the keeper of the keys.

I followed the guy out the door when I saw him leaving. He didn't even notice me, which was good on my part, but also rude, he just figured I wasn't a threat to him. If only he knew. The place the fight club was at actually wasn't that far from the party. It was deep in the woods though and I had to cut my lights off and use the guy's lights so he wouldn't know I was following him.

This...I think was the most dangerous thing I have ever done, going deep into the woods without anyone knowing where I was. I wasn't staying, I just wanted to know where it was located. When I saw the building, I turned around and left, making sure to pinpoint anything that would help me to remember the way for when I came back.

When I got back to the party it seemed as if it was right on time, I ran into Kenneth coming out of the bathroom. "Hey there, love, I was just going to come looking for you. You ready to go?"

"Sure, did you win?"

"Nope. But I only lost about two thousand before I called it quits."
I was happy for it. I had a bunch of planning to do. Time to start my workout routine back up. I need to get prepared for any fights I might get. I will not go back until I'm prepared properly.

The first thing I needed to do was research. I had no idea what MMA fighting consisted of. I'm on the master level in Jiu-Jitsu, but only entry-level in the kickboxing class I have been taking since being at school. I guess that would have something to do with more partying and less class. That will change immediately. Watching these videos helped me to realize how serious it is and dangerous.

A person not blocking correctly can be seriously injured. Increase my attendance to my kickboxing class – check, find an off-campus gym to practice in – check, get the equipment I need, and find a place to store them, soon.

# CHAPTER 3

The first part of getting my body in shape for my first fight was to increase my running time. I started getting up at four a.m.. and running four miles a day, two out and two back, and then running again in the evening at six p.m..

I went to the gym three times a week where I did jump roping to work on my cardio. The hardest part was trying to seem like the same old me when around Rosie and them.

They know I'm a junk food junkie, but you can't be a junk food junkie and do MMA. It is so hard trying to eat right when we hang out, they continue to say something snarky about what I'm eating. I decided it would be easier to just not go with them when food is involved. Which was easy when you had a guy you could use as an excuse.

Kenneth wanted me to hang with him some days during the week, this was new, and it was starting to rub me the wrong way. In all the time we have been hanging out with each other it has never been during the week, only on the weekend and that consisted mostly of going to parties, movies sometimes, lunch in the cafeteria a bunch of times, lunch in town sometimes, and I can count on my one hand how many times we have gone out to dinner.

So what was up with him now? He couldn't know what I was doing. I did tell him I was back running, only because I wanted a running partner. He informed me that I was crazy with the time I ran and declined. Too early and during prime time money time. His words.

It doesn't matter nothing is going to detour me from getting into the one thing I know will help me to rid my body of the stress of not being nothing but a dud. I'll own this sport and make it mine, something outside of my family and friends.

The following week I had completed my list. I found a gym and was able to obtain a locker there to keep my stuff, and the best part was it's not that far from where the fights are held, which would also help me with time when I need to get back to school after a fight.

The hardest part of the training was trying to find someone to spar with. The gym was made up of guys who were either too afraid to hit a girl or too chivalrous. Unless I find someone to spar with all of this is useless.

After two weeks of going to the gym, I finally found a guy who said he would not only spar with me he would train me. He told me that he noticed me and the fact that I was not giving up on my training regardless of not having anyone to spar with made him feel sorry for me enough to lend a hand, he looked to be around my age, his name was Gavin, he did not go to school.

He co-owned this gym with his bestfriend. He made sure to tell me he was not going to hold back, if I stepped in the ring with a guy then I should prepare myself to get hit by a guy.

The first two days were the worst. I left out of there sore, even my Fae healing didn't account for aches and pains. I didn't know how much longer I could take him hitting, kicking, and punching me. The worst was the same move I kept falling for and he would sweep my legs and down I would go like a pancake. His Jiu-Jitsu was better than mine and my kickboxing against him was like kicking a brick.

One time I thought I had broken my foot I tried to kick him in the ribs. He kept reminding me that he was a guy and a female would be different. He did put me on a regime of weight lifting.

Now I stand 5'4' and weigh about a hundred pounds soaking wet, and he wants me to lift weights. I'm serious about this and getting into shape, so I have to do what I have to do but lifting weights I'll have to think about that.

23

This weekend I'll be going back to the place to check it out and see how I can get on the roster. I tried to keep my ear to the people around me at the gym to see if any of them went but no one ever mentioned it. I figured they were too busy training and not talking. In two days I'll be going inside to check out the fighting first hand.

I told Kenneth that I was hanging with Rosie this Saturday and of course I told Rosie I was busy with Kenneth. That will be my routine every Saturday from this day forward. Which means I'll have to give Kenneth Sundays which I'll hate to do. That is usually my rest day for the week, I can give the fam and friends Friday.

So the first night that I went to the place where the fights were being held it was overwhelming. Watching an MMA fight online or on television is nothing compared to in person. There is more blood, the sound of the hits are amplified.

At least they are in this warehouse. The club was inside an old warehouse that looked like nothing on the outside, it looked abandoned, but when you walked inside the lights were high, and the noise was loud.

There were bleachers along the walls going in a circle with a ring in the middle of the floor surrounded by a cage.
So...underground cage MMA fighting. I decided to just take a seat up top so I can see how things were running. I wouldn't want to get myself into something unsanctioned and life-threatening.

After a few rounds of the men fights, from what I can tell, you give your name to a guy that is standing in front of a chalkboard. Then you go to the back where it looks like rooms are. I'm guessing those are dressing rooms or waiting rooms.

Probably a place to get taped.  No matter how hard I tried I could never hear much of what a guy who was standing beside the cage talking to the fighters was saying.

So it looked like I would be staying until the end so I can talk to the guy that looked in charge. The women's matches were more lethal than men. I guess they figured they had something to prove so they had to go harder.

There was one female named 'Death' and I understood why after her match.  She didn't just win she tried to bring her opponent to the brink of death. If not for a referee being in the cage I didn't think the girls she was fighting would have survived. I would never want to get in the ring with her. She was at least 6 feet tall and about two hundred and twenty pounds.

As I was sitting in the stands, I didn't know if she smelt my fear or read my mind, but it seemed as if a beam of light was shining right on me because when she was getting out the cage she looked right at me and gave me a predatory smirk.

Since I was new here and knew she shouldn't have a problem with me so soon. I couldn't help but look behind me to see if someone was sitting there. They weren't. By the time I had turned my head around, she was gone. Wow, what was that about? I wondered.

After it was all done I checked my watch, it was two a.m.. That's also good to know, how long I would probably be gone on fight nights. I stayed around waiting for everyone to be paid out and leave before approaching Joe, I found out that was the guy's name.

He announced the fighters before their fights.  I was leaning against the wall trying not to be in anyone business. That was one easy way to get hurt in places like this I would wager. After the last person walked away I straightened up.

25

"I'm guessing you want to talk to me about something since your still here, I have never seen you before, and you're not a gambler since you didn't put down any bets. So the only thing I could think of is you think you're talented enough to get in the cage?"

Before I could answer he started his spill. "You provide your gear." Which means I need to get me some tape, a mouth guard, towels, and a water bottle.

"The buy-in goes according to your skill level, looking at you I'll say amateur, which will be in the low fighting class, so the buy-in is two hundred dollars if you win you get seventy percent of the winnings with the housekeeping thirty, and that is for all classes so no worries your cut is less than others.

If, and that's a big fat if looking at you." What a way to offend a person. "You advance, the price of the buy-in goes up one hundred dollars for each class.

He told me they provide a tape man, it ensures no one is cheating so their guy tapes everyone. "There's a booklet at the door that gives all the rules and regulations of these fights. We may not be sanctioned but we have pride in what we do here.

That is how we stay off the police radar. We don't leave bodies. One main thing to know, if you seriously injure someone you will be banned from fighting, at least from here."

What the heck did they consider serious because 'Death' should never be able to fight again, she was deadly. "Last thing, we don't like easy wins or losses, if you can't hold your own in the cage and last at least past the second round then you will be asked to not return until you improve.

If you make side bets that's your business if you get paid or not, we don't care and we don't get involved. However, any squabbles are done in the ring or out the door. If I forgot anything you will learn with trial and error. Now get out, I want to lock up and get home." And with that, he walked away.

Even if I did have any questions he was not going to be the one answering them. I took the rule book he told me about on my way out the door, looking back I noticed him looking at me shaking his head.

If his view of me was anything to go by then I was going to be extremely underestimated. People always look at my height and think I'm a little bitty thing that shouldn't be even tying her shoes.

Well, I have a lot of fight in me, and if I don't know how to do anything I know how to use my small height to my advantage. I'll climb these idiots like a spider-monkey and bring them down a peg or two. Looking at the rules it was pretty straight forward, everything he said with a little added on. No biting, hitting in the privates, weapons, or shifting out if you're a shifter.

There was a list of the fighters and their skill level. I looked for 'Death' and was happy to know that I would not ever fight her, she's a gorilla shifter. Now I know why she was so aggressive, which means the person she was fighting was also a shifter.

That made me feel a little better about the situation, they heal quickly. Of course, I was putting down human since there was no way I could tell them I was other.

Which is listed on here human, shifter, other. Looking down the list it was hard to know if I knew anyone since they only had their cage name listed. By the time I got back to the dorms, it was four in the morning. This is the reason I wanted to have my Sundays to regroup.

27

It's going to be worse once I start competing. Hanging with Kenneth tonight is going to drag me down even further for classes. I showered and climbed in bed thinking about a cage name. Underestimated, short and fierce, victim maker. I fell asleep thinking how hard this was going to be.

When I awoke and turned my head to check my phone I noticed that even though I tried I didn't sleep the entire day away. It was eleven o'clock and I had missed three texts from Kenneth asking if I wanted to meet up for lunch in the downstairs lunchroom. I flipped over on my back deciding to welcome my fate of having to get out of the bed.

I texted him back telling him I had just woken up and I would be down there as soon as I took a quick shower. By the time I got to the lunchroom, he was already there with enough food in front of him to feed an entire team of people. "I didn't know what you would want so I just got one of everything. What you don't eat I'll make sure to take care of."

I kissed him on the cheek. "Thanks, babe." I found that I was hungrier than I thought I would be.

"If I didn't know better I would think that you were pregnant. Since I know you're a virgin I'm not worried about how much you slept today and eating right now."

I stuck my tongue out at him. "I missed breakfast, and I guess the early morning running is catching up with me. I needed to catch up on sleep, so back off."

He put up his hands palms up and gave me a sheepish smile. "After we eat I thought we could catch an early movie. Since we both have Chem in the morning, so I want to get back early and do a little studying for the pop quiz and figured you would need to do the same." Thank goodness for small mercies.

"I completely forgot about that pop quiz. Good thing I have you around. What movie did you want to see?"

"It doesn't matter, your pick."

"Okay, what is this. You have never let me pick a movie too scared I was going to pick a love story."

"I'm trying to be more open. Your pick." After the movie, which was an action movie his favorite. I'm going to hit him with a romance next time. I went back to my room to do some needed studying, I made sure to close my door and hang my studying in session sign on the outside so nobody would bother me.

When my Monday alarm went off on my phone I awoke to my face plastered to my Chem book. Good thing for recurring alarms or this day could have started much worse.

When I arrived at Chemistry class Kenneth was already there in our usual area. I flopped down beside him. "How did your studying go? I don't know for sure about myself. I just know I awoke with my face in my book."

"It went good, I got a lot of studying done, I think I'm over ready." Surprisingly enough I was shocked to know I knew more than I thought I did. If I have to say so myself I would say I aced it. All that worrying for nothing.

"Want me to walk you to your next class? This was it for me." Asked Kenneth.

"Sure if you want to, that would be great."

"What do you have going on this week?"

"Just the usual classes, doing my running. I missed my morning run, but I'll do my evening run. Did you want to join me?"

"Running and not in my wolf form and on purpose, I think I'll take a pass babe."

"Okay, well how about meeting me in the gym at two to work out?"

He stopped walking and touched my arm so I did too. "Rosalyn, what's going on? You know you can tell me anything. Right? What's up with all of the working out and running?"

I continued walking. I didn't want to look at him when I attempted at squirting the truth. I hate that Fae can't lie, we can give vague answers, but never lie to keep us honest. "I don't have the slightest idea what you're talking about."

"You've stopped hanging out and partying, I can't remember the last time I have seen you take a drink. Your eating has changed from junk food junkie to health nut, your exercising, running, and even lifting weights. You don't think I noticed but you've even started religiously doing your kickboxing again."

"Are you stalking me? How do you know I'm kickboxing?"

"Ummm, sweetie I introduced you to it remember. I take the class also. The instructor wanted to know if we wanted to take advantage of the couple's class at a discount since you were back coming also. Imagine my surprise with that since we used to do the class together but you said it was hard and stopped."

I ignored that snipe, "I would love to do the couples class with you. I don't mind the partying. Tell me when the next Friday party is and I'm there. Also, my eating is different because it's better for my body. You should want a healthy girlfriend dude. Stop giving me a hard time."

"I'm seeing something that's not here. Aren't I? My apologies. Couples kickboxing, I'll sign us up and let you know when the first class is."

30

"Wonderful. Now let me get inside this class so the professor stops giving me the stink eye and the class hasn't even started yet." One good thing that came out of this is I get a strong partner for kickboxing which will work in my benefit. My legs are going to be so strong after practicing with Kenneth that after I kick a female she won't know what hit her.

## CHAPTER 4

When I thought I was ready I went back to the club to try my hand at my first fight. I was nervous, extremely nervous. I had never fought anyone in my life. So going in a cage on my own free will and fighting seemed a new level to me. When I approached the guy that had talked at me that night I came, he looked surprised to see me.

"Huh, I didn't think you would be back. I guess not everyone has brains. It's your life. Take these forms and fill them out. If it's a blank spot then you will not fight. When you are done return them to me with your money."

The forms were medical history, the release of responsibility stating I'll not hold anyone here or anyone associated with this outfit responsible for any injuries I inquire. Emergency contact. Oh my goodness. Who could I possibly put down without getting busted if they were needed to be called?

I don't know why she came to mind but I put my cousin Randa down. She would definitely keep my secret if it came to it. There's also a form here that asks what my name was going to be. I still haven't thought about it that long so I put the first thing that came to mind on the paper. Vengeance.

I sat in the spot I sat the very first night I came here. It seemed as if everyone else liked to sit closer to the cages, and the first row around the cage was for the fighters, their coaches if they had one and their stuff.

I didn't have much stuff, tape, mouth guard, and gloves. What more did I need? I came dressed for my fight and had a change of clothes in the car that I will change into after I left.

When I returned the paperwork to Joe he looked at the cage name I put down looked me up and down, laughed, and handed me a ticket. "Take that to the guy over there by the chalkboard and pull a name, that is who you will be fighting tonight." He started walking away, "Good luck...Vengeance." He said mockingly.

I'll show him. I might be small but I have the skill and I'm powerful. When it was my time to go into the cage I was a nervous wreck. I was so shaky getting taped that the guy told me that if I was that nervous then just maybe this was not the sport for me and I should go home.

That gave me pause, and I stopped at least until my name was announced, which made the shakes come back in full force. When going in a fight I would assume that a person has to have some sort of state of mind, also I would think that the last thing a person needs is for the spectators to see you and start laughing at your cage name.

What they didn't know was I could hear them and their snide remarks. "That's Vengeance? Ha! more like scrawny." "She is going to be destroyed." "I can't believe they will allow someone that small to get in the cage." "I hope she has insurance." And it went on, to the point that I had to force myself to tune it out if I didn't want their words to sike me out of my fight.

You can do this ... you can do this. You have trained for this you have kicked man butt. You can fight. I gave myself a Pep talk as I stood in the middle of the cage awaiting my opponent. When she arrived it made me feel a little better, she looked to be only a few inches taller than me and her statue was maybe fifty pounds thicker.

She was human so I couldn't use my Fae strength. At the start of the fight, we just circled each other at first. I figured that she was waiting for me to attack so she could see my technique. I didn't let her down, I attacked her with full force.

We were somewhat matched except she had experience and knew what to do and when to do it. I, on the other hand, knew nothing. By the end of the fifth round, I had lost. But I felt good about that loss. I held my own and it was my first battle.

I was down two hundred dollars but that was okay, the experience alone, with the moves that she did and I couldn't counter allowed me to see what I need to work on and what I would need to do my next match.

I didn't stick around after my match. I was exhausted and I had a date with Kenneth the next day and if I canceled again he would start to get suspicious. When I got back to the room it was kind of early so I wasn't surprised to see the girls sitting around. "Hey, guys what are you three up to?"

"Nothing really," replied Rosie. "I was waiting on the guys to come back. Where going downstairs to the common area to watch a movie if you want to join us. We have pizza on the way." I was still sweaty and sticky from my fight since I didn't take a shower.

But it did sound like fun lying back watching a movie. "Sure, that sounds great. I'm going to go grab a shower and meet you all down there if you're gone already."

I went to my room to grab some jogging pants and a tee-shirt then headed to the shower hall. While I was in there I closed my eyes for a second enjoying the spray of the water on my back. I don't know if a person can fall asleep standing up, but I swear when I opened my eyes I felt as if I was waking up.

I washed up as fast as I could and went to the room to return my shower items. The place was empty so I just headed downstairs. Everyone was there and they all seemed happy to see me, even the girlfriends. I texted Kenneth and told him what was going on if he wanted to join us.

Halfway through the movie Kenneth still wasn't there. I didn't expect him to show up, it just would have been nice if he would have. I guess it didn't matter one way or the other because the next thing I knew someone was shaking me. "You fell asleep, good thing you don't snore." Commented Sapphire.

"Hey sis, when did you get here?"

"When the movie was close to the end, I decided to stick around and watch the rest."

I stood up and stretched. "It's good seeing you, we're at the same school and barely see each other."

"I know but we are in different years and we have different friends. So."

"Well, I'm going to head on up to my room. By the way. Why do you have on gloves?" She looked startled that I would notice that and ask, I could see her mind going. I knew that look. She was trying to figure out what to say since she couldn't lie.

Which told me whatever it was she didn't want to share. "Never mind, it's not that important." I lowered my voice. "Keep your secrets, it won't hurt my feelings. Trust me I have my own secrets I wouldn't be willing to share." She gave me a small smile, hugged me, and walked out of the building.

"I change my mind. I'm going to go over to the cafeteria and see if there is any food out that could be snatched up. I'm starving."

34

Theresa looked at me, "well if you would have eaten more than one slice of pizza you wouldn't be."

"One slice is enough. I'm talking about healthy food. Later squares." I called as I walked away. When I entered the big cafeteria the only thing I could see left out was the salad bar, which was fine with me. By the time I made the biggest salad I could put on the plate and sat down, everyone else was also in there making them a big salad.

When I was halfway through my salad Kenneth walked into the room, he made him a plate also and joined me at the table. "I wish I would have been able to make it for the movie. I didn't get your message until I was walking in the door after I cut my phone back on.

I had a big job to do tonight and one thing my boss hates is when our phone vibrates or rings while he is giving instructions. After that, I forgot to cut it back on. Forgive me?" He looked at me with sappy eyes and his lip poked out.

"Of course I forgive you. Work is work babe, and nothing comes between a man and his money. However, you only have until I finish my salad then I'm headed to bed. By the way, what are we doing tomorrow?"

"About that. You're not going to like what I have to say, but I have to work tomorrow. I'll be heading to Delaware and won't be back until late Monday evening."

"What about your Monday class?"

"I already checked the college board and all we have to do for Chem class is computing four formulas, which the professor is probably going to demonstrate tomorrow in class. I figured I could just look at your notes and be all good. If nothing else you take explicit notes."

"I got you." I was not going to argue, being able to sleep in tomorrow, it couldn't have worked out better if I had planned it myself. The next day when I woke up it was six o'clock in the evening. I knew I was tired but I couldn't have ever imagined I was running off fumes. When I stumbled out the room the sitting area was empty.

I went to the mini-fridge we had to grab a yogurt. Then I grabbed my stuff and headed to the bathroom. I brushed my teeth, washed my face, changed clothes, popped open my yogurt, and headed downstairs to the lunchroom.

I grabbed a quick veggie burger, sweet potato fries, and some water and headed out the door. I ate as I walked to the gym building. I needed to get in some weight lifting as prescribed by my trainer. I have to bulk up if I'm going to use only human strength. During my fight, I noticed that my hits as a human did nothing to my opponent.

After I did the workout that was on my phone sent from my trainer Gavin I returned to the room to find it still empty. I tapped on Rosie's door, no answer. I guess they went out with their guys. I went to my room to get a head start on the next day's lesson. After reading for an hour I decided to just go to bed.

When someone is depending on you to take expert notes that is what you are supposed to be focused on. I, however, could only focus on my fight and how to improve on the next one. I did get some notes just not everything I usually would get. To cover myself I just took pictures of the board and wrote down keynotes of what the professor said.

At least it was something. I'll join tonight's study session get the notes I missed and he won't question me on what was on my mind that I missed taking notes. Now with that settled. I'm going to skip my next class and do some review of fights to try to get some good moves that I may be able to use in my next match.

I was so wrapped up in watching fights and looking up moves I didn't realize until my alarm went off telling me that it was time for that study group I had missed the entire day of classes. It was now five o'clock. I ran over to the big library while running through my mind rather or not I missed anything important today, I don't think I did. I know I had clinicals today.

We're allowed to miss two and this is my first so I'm good with that. Then there is biology, and who wouldn't want to miss that? I think dissection was today. I can catch up on that. I'm all good.

When I entered the library my stomach took that moment to protest. Oh yeah, that is the one thing I forgot, food. Well, it's too late now I have to do this study group for the notes. It should be quick and then I'll go to the cafeteria before they close at ten.

After the study session that in my mind took way to long, I ran to the cafeteria, I think my stomach constantly growling was a big reason why they ended it when they did. Don't matter I got the notes I needed.

When I entered the cafeteria the last person I wanted to see was in there. My sister. If I wasn't so hungry I would turn right around. After getting my food I joined her at her table, if I didn't she would just make a huge deal about it later in the room. "Hey." That was all I got out before I dove into my food.

"It's not good to miss meals to the point of starvation where you can't even take a breath in-between bites."

"Hmmm." I had no time to talk, I hadn't eaten and if she thought her comments were going to slow me down she is clearly misguided. After I had my fill I put my fork down and leaned back. "Look, Rosie, do I bother you when you're eating? Let me answer that for you, No, so back off."

She raised her hands in the air, "testy, testy. You must have been busy today because you didn't make lunch with us."

37

"Yes, I was studying and lost track of time, well worth it."

"That's good to hear, you were missing this weekend, and I know you are tired of me riding you but I just assumed you were back to partying with Kenneth."

"I caught up on sleep this weekend. And like I told you before, what I do and don't do with Kenneth is none of your business. You're my sister, you're not my keeper. If I want to party then that is what I'll do. Back off Rosie on the need to interfere in my life before I welcome myself into yours with Augustas." I stood up ready to leave, "I guess I'll be missing another meal with you since I just lost my appetite for the rest of my food."

I was not going back to the room and have to deal with her. Kenneth had not called me to say he was back. I called an Uber to go to the gym for a late-night sparring match to release some tension. I was hoping that Gavin would be there. When I arrived at the gym I was kinda shocked how many cars were in the parking lot.

When I went inside I noticed about eight people from the club that was there working out. So this is when they all come, at night. I stood back and watched a few sparring runs to get some tips.

While I was sitting there Gavin approached me, "I came to your first fight, I have a plan put together for areas that you need to improve on. Also, I hope that you are doing your weight lifting regimen because I have increased it by ten pounds and five reps. I know you're a girl but in the cage, I don't want you hitting like one, you're weak."

"Well, thanks for that."

"Hey, I'm here to give you your money's worth."

"Anything I can work on tonight? I could use a stress release."

"Hit the weights and then the bag with punches and kicks. Do the flex workout and you should be good."

"Got it. Thanks, Gavin."

After my workout, I felt a little better. When I picked up my phone I had a missed message from Kenneth telling me that he will be back in the morning, a message from Rosie apologizing and saying it was safe to come to the room now, I even received a message from Danielle telling me that my sister didn't mean any harm and she wasn't lying, it's safe to return to the room.

I called myself an Uber and by the time I got back to campus, it was two in the morning. One thing to be happy about the time is everyone was asleep. I grabbed a quick shower and climbed into bed.

As soon as my head hit the pillow I was out. The next morning I walked out of the room and before anyone could say anything I told them it was all water under the bridge and we should just move forward.

# CHAPTER 5

It had been a couple of weeks of training, hanging with Kenneth, school, hanging with my crew, going to the school gym to lift, going for my training, running day, and evening. I was being pulled very thin in too many directions.

I fight tonight and Rosie and the crew are determined that I go with them to this play that is being put on by the school's drama club. Since Kamaray is involved.

I adore Kamaray a bunch, but there is no way I'm not going to the club tonight for my match. He will have to understand if I duck out early, which means I can't go with everyone because if I sit by them then they will hound me when I get ready to leave.

"Rosalyn we're about the head out. Come on we're all going together," Rosie said sticking her head in my bedroom.

I raised the book I was reading, "I have one more chapter to read. It's still early yet. I'll meet you all there and find you."

"Seriously. When have you ever been this dedicated?"

"Would you make up your mind, at first I'm not studious enough, now I'm too studious. You can't have it both ways just to fit your narrative."

She stepped into my room and leaned on the side of my dresser. "You're right and I'm sorry, I know I have been riding you like crazy lately and it's not fair. I guess I have a lot of stuff on my mind, weird things have been happening."

"What weird things?" She may annoy me but she is still my sister.

"Nothing. Forget I brought it up. We'll be waiting for you in the auditorium."

"Cool."

After they all left, I closed my door. I would give them fifteen minutes to get there, another ten to find a seat. I know what door they are going in so I'll just pretend to forget and go to a different one. I'll text them and tell them I don't see them.

Relay what door I came in, convince them not to come to me, then wave my hand to show them where I'm at. I'll stay for two hours. I already have an Uber set to come and get me and get my fight on.

This is what I'm talking about I shouldn't have to go through all this just to have a day to myself to do what I want to do. When I got to the club and got signed in, I was happy that I had gotten there when I did I was the fourth to fight. This just might work out, after all, fourth to fight means I might get back in time to either catch the end of the play or find the crew in the crowd as they are exiting.

It was on fight number two and each round is ten minutes unless someone gets a tap out. If not there are five rounds then the person with the most points wins.

When my fight came I was not as nervous as I was the first time. First fight jitters are what Gavin called it when I told him how I was feeling. He said it would be different as the fights continue. I was ready for this. I have trained my butt off, I have studied, I have prepared. I'm ready for this fight.

When my opponent stepped in the cage, everything I felt went down the drain. This woman stood at least five-eight with the weight included, her freaking muscles had muscles. Okay, I can do this. I just have to make sure she doesn't hit me.

41

Kicks are fine but I need to stay away from her gloves or I'm going to be in trouble. The first round, I wanted to feel her out. Her fight stance was just like a guy I watched at the gym, I saw all his flaws and thought in my head what I would do to counterstrike his kicks and hits.

They must be related or train together. Which was good for me because by the end of the fourth round I had a tap out. I had won my match. The payout was nothing to sneeze at either.

I called the Uber as soon as I got outside, and I had to laugh at the situation. My Uber driver was actually at the fight. He was a spectator waiting for a customer. Tonight was a good night for me, I did not want to explain to my sister about my whereabouts.

I told dude he will get a twenty-dollar tip if he kept his eyes out the rearview mirror while I changed back into my clothes. Good thing for small clothes and big purses.

When I arrived back at the building I slipped inside. Looking at the program they were at the end of the play, thank goodness I didn't miss it. Thirty minutes later everyone was being let out. I was standing in the middle of the yard looking around for the group.

I text Rosie and told her where I was standing. When they joined me Rosie told me that the plan was to wait on Kamaray to change and we're all going to the Steak house to grab dinner and celebrate.

While we were walking to the vehicles Danielle strolled close to me and whispered low. "Where were you? I came over to your side looking for you and you weren't there. I even went to the bathroom and you weren't there either. I waited around for you for about ten minutes and you never came back. I had to lie to Rosie about you not wanting to move. So you owe me."

"I had something that I needed to do and I knew if I told you about it, you would give me grief about missing the play and being inconsiderate. I also didn't want to have to explain to anyone where I needed to go."

"I can understand that. Well, let me give you the highlights of what you missed. You know there will be questions. We're talking about Kamaray." And she did every tidbit.

That is the reason she is my bestfriend/sister, no explanation needed, and she always comes through in the clutch. I can honestly say that I enjoyed myself tonight at dinner. I laughed so hard my side hurt. I do like hanging with these guys when I have the time to do so, and no one is giving me grief.

When we returned to the campus after dinner I went up to my room to get some rest. Tomorrow is Kenneth's day. I don't know what is going to be involved so I need to rest up. He never fails to impress.

Waking up the next morning I felt rejuvenated and ready for the day, I grabbed my phone opening it to a text message.

*: Hey babe don't be mad but I need to take a raincheck on tonight. I have a job to do. I've tried but I can't get out of it.*

Upset, is he crazy. That clears my day. I can go to the gym and get a few sparring rounds in.

*: Oh, no worries babe. I'll find something to occupy my time, knowing Rosie she will find something for me to do with the crew. You handle your business and I'll see you in class on Monday.*

*: You are the best girlfriend ever.*

*: And don't you forget it.*

43

Hey, no judging, he doesn't know I would rather go to the gym.

When I arrived at the gym Gavin was there as if he expected me to show up. "You finally decided to show."

"Um, did I miss something? I didn't know we had an appointment set up for today. I'm only here because my guy canceled our plans."

"Oh. So you are not serious about fighting then? My bag I thought you were wanting to be the best." With that, he turned and walked away. I jogged to catch up with his long strides.

"Wait a minute. I am serious."

"Then you should know with all this research that you told me about that a fighter always shows up the next day after a fight to get critiqued, and to work on what they did and didn't do."

"I thought that was only if I lost."

"Oh. You think you won because you won that little taste of money, and your opponent tapped out."

"Yeah."

He stopped walking and looked at me. "Sorry to bust your little happy bubble. You didn't. It took you four rounds to get that tap ... in my book you lost."

"Well Damn!" I don't usually curse, but that comment deserved it. "I bust my butt in that cage, the person was taller and bigger than me, and I had to use moves that we never worked on to pin her."

"All I hear is a bunch of excuses as to why it took you four rounds. If you are done playing with the pity party string we can get to work."

44

What could I say to that, "I'm done and ready." Now when I had lost my first match Gavin worked me to the bone, saying I would never lose another match after he is done with me. This workout was the worst. I won and I'm being put through the wringer.

By the time we were done three hours had passed and I was wondering as I laid in the middle of the ring if I was ever going to walk again. I think I was just physically punished for that win.

I walked to the car with my legs feeling like rubber. I was wondering when was my Fae side going to kick in and give me back some of the feelings I had lost an hour ago. We're stronger, more durable than humans, and even some shifters.

But even we have a pushing point, and constantly being kicked, flipped, hit, and required to lift, jump rope, and hit a punching bag will push us to the limit. I hurt everywhere. I need food so I can reenergize and soon. When I got back to campus I honestly didn't care how I looked I went straight to the cafeteria.

It was kind of crowded since it was early evening and a Sunday to boot. That didn't stop me from piling my plates up with enough food to feed a small army, and I didn't care about the looks I was getting. They can suck it. I need this food. Food means energy rejuvenation. As I was polishing off the first plate, anticipating digging into the second.

Rosie plopped down beside me with her back to the table and crossing her arms. "Since we are the same and I know what that much food means, I'm not going to assume anything when it comes to you, however, I have to ask. Are you eating like that because you gave Kenneth your cookies?"

"Cookies? What cookies?"

"You know the who-who, the secret box."

45

"Rosie are you in your weird way trying to ask me if Kenneth and I had sex?"

"Well yeah."

"You are so weird, sometimes I wonder are we related. Also, the answer to your question. I'm still a virgin."

"First off how could you wonder if were related were identical twins, secondly I'm happy to hear it. However, that gives me pause. It takes a lot for us to exert enough energy where we have to consume that much food to get it back." She said pointing at my plates.

"Um-hmm." That's all I had for her.

"That's all you got to say? You're not going to share with me what you were doing to need this much food?"

I put my fork down and looked at her. "Just know it wasn't sexual or illegal so no worries." I looked around the cafeteria. "What are you doing here? Where is everyone else?"

"Oh, well I was walking past and saw you through the window so I thought I would drop in on you. Everyone else is at the football field, you do remember that there is a game tonight and Marlo and Devon are playing.

I know you don't like football and you are usually with Kenneth on game day. However you're not right now, so how about I wait here until you get done and then you join us for one game?"

"Rosie."

"Come on. One game." She poked out her bottom lip. "Pleaaassseee. Pretty Pleassssse."

Sighing I looked at my food and then her. "Fine, but I'm finishing my food and if you think to rush me you can just go without me." Five minutes later, I tried dragging it out as long as I could. We were headed to the field.

I really don't understand football, catching a ball and running with it hoping that the person that is chasing you to hit you is slower than you. Not my idea of fun. Any other sport in the world and they decide to join the football team.

When we made it to the seats everyone was surprised to see me, especially Kamaray. "Rosalyn you came to a game, you have to come and sit by me so I can explain it to you because I know you don't know a thing about football." I laughed and sat next to him. "Where is your girl tonight? She doesn't like football either?"

"Oh no there she is right there." He pointed and I followed his finger.

"A cheerleader, really Kamaray. I never thought you were the type to go for someone superficial."

"Hey, watch what you say about my future wife, and she is not superficial."

"Your future wife. So she's your mate? And what makes you say she's not superficial?"

"No she is not my mate, and in this big old world, you are lucky to find your one true mate so you find what you can love. And would a superficial person volunteer at the soup kitchen and old folks home? She also is a member of the school's choir, and she is studying to be a radiologist technician. None of that says superficial."

47

"My apologies. I just never met a cheerleader who was not bubbly and all about themselves before. Now back to the wife thing. You do realize that she is the third wife you have had since being here. What is that one a year?"

"In my defense, I thought that every one of them was the one, it's not my fault they couldn't hang with the intensity of what is me. Karen didn't like camping, who doesn't like camping? And Sophie kept talking about herself in the third person. At first, I thought it was funny but after a while it became annoying. Sheila, on the other hand, loves camping, a matter of fact she knows more about it than me, she also likes to Fish and will clean it. You would know that if you joined us on any of our crew camping trips."

I started to reply but he waved his hand. "I digress, I know you still like us, no worries. Also speaking of. You always say we never give you a warning. So here it is. In two weeks from today 'that is two weeks' we will be doing a camping weekend and I expect you to be there with or without Kenneth. Got it."

"Kamaray."

"Don't you Kamaray me. There is no room in this conversation for a no. Again I ask, got it?"

"Yes, for you I'll go." Darn it. Well, that is one weekend I'll make sure not to put my name in for a match. How do I supposed to get any better if I have to miss training and matches to hang with them? Not alone darn it. I text Kenneth and told him about the trip.

I also informed him that if being my boyfriend isn't an option then missing this trip isn't one. This one weekend he will choose between me and partying. We will be stuck together.

I cheered whenever they did, I hollered when they hollered. Kamaray did what he said and explained every term, move, and flag. Devon made a touchdown, and Marlo was on the field to hit people, which he did a lot. I would like to say that I enjoyed myself, but nope I didn't and when it was over I think I shouted louder than anyone else except I did it for a different reason.

I was ready to go. Everyone said they were going to grab some food. I told them I was tired and was going to head back to the room. A football game is different than dinner, and me feeling like a fifth wheel. No thanks.

I returned to the room and laid back on my bed. I still haven't gotten a text back from Kenneth concerning my request. Answer or no, he got the message. Tomorrow after class I'll have to go and refresh my camping stuff.

Just in case Kenneth does come I'm going to grab a family tent. That way he will have his part and I'll have my part. We can be together without him thinking he is going to get lucky.

I also need a porta-potty because I'm not going in the woods, I hated going in the woods. I'm also going to get one of those camping sinks so I can wash up and brush my teeth and not at the stream, a water heater to warm up the water I collect, and better sleeping bags, mine feels like I'm on the ground and I know Kenneth is not going to get him one because he doesn't know the first thing about camping.

The way I figure it if I make sure he has the best time of his life then he will be willing to go again and that time without complaint.

⊕

Gavin once told me that a fighter shouldn't fight two weekends in a row, but he didn't take into account a fighter who's family and friends were forcing her to go camping. So I'll be fighting this weekend and camping the next.

49

When I arrived at the warehouse I looked around first to make sure that Gavin was not there.

The last thing I need is for him to give me crap. When I walked up to Joe he looked at me and shook his head. "I know what you are going to say, but I have a thing next weekend so this weekend is my time. If I skip two weekends my timing will be off."

"You know what the buy-in is and you know the process so get going. It must be your lucky night also, we have only one fighter for you so no need to draw tonight, and to make it even better. You are the first fight. Good luck with that."

Two or three things happened that were out of my control. The first was the person I was fighting she was not a person I would hope to fight. She was at least five-eleven and was so stocked it was unbelievable, the other thing that happened was she was nowhere near my weight class. And the last thing that happened was I got beat.

There was no competition given on my end. The only thing I was able to do was duck and swing when I could. The only thing that was in my control was the fact that I lasted for four rounds and lost. When I say I lost, I lost big time. Let's just say when I awoke I was in the infirmary.

"So you got knocked out big time. I was shocked that you lasted as long as you did, with who you were in there with. Since I know that you are alive I'm going to get back out there."

"Thanks, Joe. I really do appreciate it." I don't understand how they could put me in the cage with a bigfoot behemoth. At least I learned some new things while observing her technique. It would have been better if I won.

If Gavin finds out about this fight I can only imagine what he will put me through in training. I stayed there for about fifteen more minutes before gathering my stuff and leaving. I was amazed at how many people complimented me on doing a good job as I headed out the door.

One guy even said I lost him a bunch of money because he bet that I would go down in the first round. That made me feel a little better about the loss.

When I got back to the room everyone was there. I wanted to scream and pull my hair out because all I wanted to do was take a shower and go lay down. But it seems that my bad luck from the cage followed me back to school. As soon as I returned from the shower they were on me.

"Ros, we just put in a movie, and since it has been many moons since you have chilled with us and watched a movie you owe us a night." Stated Danielle.

"Fine, but if I fall asleep don't be upset."

Theresa laughed, "you say that every time and be the last to go to bed even when the movie is over."

"Don't say I didn't warn you," I remember seeing the title of the movie and I remember hearing Danielle ask me if I wanted some popcorn. And then there was nothing. The next thing I know I was waking up to an empty room. Those slags left me here sleep and went to bed. I told them I was tired, they never listen.

# CHAPTER 6

One thing that I have realized in my life is time flies when you are facing doing something that you don't want to do. If I was going to be doing something fun this week would have crept past at a snail's crawl. Right now I'm standing outside at the crack of dawn on a Friday morning watching everyone load up for our family and friend camping trip.
I would rather be in bed and the way that Kenneth is looking at me he feels the same way.

Laying my head on his shoulder I told him. "As soon as we pitch our tent we can go back to sleep." He just gave me a very unfriendly look. With that, I straightened up. "Kenneth, I take it back. I don't want to ruin everyone's weekend. So forget what I said. You don't have to go, your off the hook." Kissing him on the lips to show him I had no hard feelings. "I don't want you to be in a mood all weekend, then I'm going to be in a mood. And that's not going to be good for anyone. I'll talk to you on Monday when we return." And with that, I walked away.

Camping is not for everyone. I know this, but when you in a relationship you compromise with your partner. I, however, am not his forever girl so what does it matter.

If he wants to spend time with me doing something I want to do then he can and if not I refuse to force him to. I walked up to Rosie and Augustas. "I'm going to ride with you guys. Kenneth's going to stay here."

Rosie looked at me, "What! After all that stuff you bought."

"Rosie doesn't. He doesn't know what I bought and he doesn't want to go. Please just leave it, unless you decided you don't care if I go. Because if you make a scene I'll be going back to my room and my bed."

She huffed so loud I was surprised a booger didn't fly out her nose. "Fine. I can be civilized. Just so you know I'm starting to dislike him, more and more."

I didn't want to hear her complain about Kenneth so I jumped in the backseat and closed the door waiting for them to finish packing up. I figured I would just close my eyes and sleep all the way there. Before closing my eyes I looked out the window and Kenneth was nowhere to be seen. Huh, I honestly hoped. I guess that's that.

When we got to the campground since Kenneth was not there. Kamaray and Devon helped me lug all my stuff up the trail. Another thing I didn't like about these camping trips is there is no parking near the camping area. You park in a lot and then walk a trail for about three miles until you come to the campsite. Another thing I don't like is the no cell phones rule.

Everyone puts their cell phone in a locked box that Augustas would carry and keep in a secret location to only be pulled out in case of an emergency. Then there is the participation rule. You must participate in every activity. We are here to do bonding and spend time together.

If we wanted to spend time apart we could have just stayed at the school. Blah Blah Blah. Well, I don't dislike that rule. The guys are coming up with some fun activities for us to do.

When we finally made it to the campground I was happy to get my tent set up so I could lay back and relax a little until everyone was done. My tent was a popup tent so I didn't have much to do. Instead of outside where it was going to be initially I set up Kenneth's supposed to be room as my bathroom. I went to the lake and filled up the container I bought for heating water.

I set it out.  When the campfire was made the heat should heat the water. At least that's what I hoped for. You would usually use the sun, but since this was the middle of fall and we're in the woods the sun is limited.

Did I mention that I brought a cot with me to lay the sleeping bag on? Well, I did. One for the both of us. I'm using his as a dresser so I don't have to keep pulling my clothes out my bag. I was laid back awaiting the first thing we were going to do on this fine Friday. I was dozing off which is a bad thing with this group. When I heard the call.

"The last tent is up." I knew what that meant.

"So what are we doing first?" I called out upon exiting my tent. Since I was single bound I pitched it close to camp. Not that I needed that much privacy either way.

Devon picked me up and swung me around, "it's so good you decided to join us again Ros, you are missed on our family trips. And to answer your question. We will be Fishing off the pier."

They have got to be kidding. Why in tarnation can't we Fish from here? The freaking pier is a twenty-minute walk one way. "Yippee. I love Fishing." Hate the walking though. Taking a deep breath and telling myself.

You will enjoy this weekend, so suck it up buttercup. With that, I went to my tent and grabbed my two Fishing poles and tackle box, took a seat by the fire to wait for everyone else so we could head out.

I find myself being a likable person. I also generally like everyone. Now with that being said, there has to be something sneaky and slimy about Bloom's girlfriend because not only does she rub me the wrong way, her voice is annoying. It has a high pitch squeak to it that I swear is made up. No one talks like that in real life.

54

She is always correcting him on everything that he does. No Bloom, the chairs should be facing sideways so we are not directly facing the fire. No Bloom, there is no need to take all three of your Fishing poles your only one person. No Bloom, you shouldn't have juice right now with this hike water is best.

Bloom put on a hat it doesn't matter if you're a shifter and run hot. Bloom this, Bloom that. I'm on the verge of paying Theresa to put a hex on her. Nothing serious. Something like giving her strep-throat so she can't talk the rest of the trip.

Bloom's girlfriend. Freida is her name turned to me, "I haven't seen you around before, and this is my second camping trip with everyone. You and Rosie must be related? You two look so much alike."

"They're identical twins sweetheart," Bloom answered for me giving me a weak smile.

I just looked at her and slowed down so I was no longer walking beside them. I don't know what had gotten into me walking that fast to even have to interact with her at all. "Hey everyone. I got a hiking game we can play." I called out.

Rosie looked at me and raised an eyebrow, "and what my dear sister is that?"

"The quiet game. Let's see who can stay quiet until we get to the pier. The person that wins don't have to pull a straw to clean the Fish and the person the loses automatically have to clean the fish that is caught and everyone else is off the hook." That'll shut her up because everyone agreed but her. Of course, she would disagree she hasn't stopped talking.

When we got to the pier I was smiling from ear to ear. One guess on who is cleaning all Fish that are caught. Even after saying one more time, three times. Sucks to be her. She is currently trying to convince Bloom to do it for her. But as she has been told several times.

Loses or wins in games cannot be passed on to the next person regardless of their station in your life. I was enjoying this a little too much and Danielle and Theresa told me as much. As which I reminded them that they forced me on this trip not the other way around and I needed to get my jollies somehow.

When we arrived back at the camp with our six Fish, yes six, which didn't matter because I knew Bloom would break the rule for miss "What about my manicure?" In which I replied, "No worries dear we have gloves for that, it saves your hands from the Fish smell."

She did not appreciate my help. As I was saying, when we arrived back at the camp a guy was sitting at our fire. I was in the back and gauged everyone before taking a fighting stance. I knew something was up when Rosie looked at me and grinned. I did the tangle eye look at her.

Augustas walked over to him. "Hey, Neko."

"What up, you failed to tell me how far I would have to walk to get to camp. And then when I got here and no one was here I was quite worried for a minute. But I'm here now."

"Well, I'm glad you made it. Rosalyn this is my good friend Neko."
I looked at him, then Neko, then Rosie. "And."

Rosie popped my arm, "he's here so he can be your second, that way you don't have to sit out on group activities. He never came before because he didn't want to feel left out this was the perfect time for him to join us also."

"What would he had done if Kenneth would have come?"

"Girl bye, you know darn well he wasn't coming camping."

"I didn't know no such thing. I guess as long as you two aren't trying to play matchmaker."
Augustas threw his arm around my shoulder, "Now Ros you know we wouldn't do that."

"Just making sure." I walked up to him and shook his hand. "I guess you're my game partner for this weekend, I'm Rosalyn by the way."

"Nice to meet you. I hope I don't let you down."

Devon came over, "we're going to toast some marshmallows while Freida cleans the fish. Then when she is done we're going to do a team scavenger hunt. The team that wins will get this bottle of whiskey that will be used for the game we are playing tomorrow night."

Everyone received a list with pictures and a basket. There were different plants and flowers that we had to find and put in the basket. Who do I look like a gardener? I was happy my teammate was excited to get started.

Augustas passed out mini timers, "everyone set your timer you have one hour and whatever you've found that is it. Everyone has to be back at camp by the time the timer goes off or you automatically lose...Alright everyone, on ya mark, get set, and hunt."

We all took off in different directions. When we got in the woods I turned to Neko, "do you want to divide and conqueror stick together and take our chances?"

"Let's work together that way we don't lose time finding each other when time is almost done."

57

"Cool."

And with that, we were off. I never thought I would have so much fun running through the woods looking for plants and flowers. There were twenty items on the list and we found eight. We had ten minutes to get back to camp we were running and laughing so hard when we burst through the trees the alarm had just started. Everyone made it back in time. The only person that didn't have any items in their basket was Bloom.

"Bloom, what happened?"

"Oh nothing, it was hard for Freida to get around in the woods."

"Whoever thought it would be fun to run around in the woods and get hit in the face with tree branches and stumble everywhere have a bad sense of fun." Commented Freida.

There was so much I could have said but I decided to enjoy my weekend and let it go. Why would a person come camping that doesn't like the woods? I don't come camping because I always have to sit out the games unless it's individual or one of the girlfriends isn't feeling well.

After everyone's items were counted the winner was Devon and his girl Lorraine found twelve items. They know their stuff. When I was looking at them and noticed how they interacted with each other. I think they are true mates because he hasn't let her out of his sight since he ran into her Sophomore year. I was happy for them.

As always there was group cooking. Everyone participated and we chatted and talked about our adventure of trying to find the items on the list. Augustas, Bloom, and Kamaray ended up recleaning the Fish unless we wanted to eat scales and all.

I hate to say it but unless she is his mate I don't see her lasting until senior year. Bloom may be a human, but he loves camping and being in the woods. I don't see him settling for someone that is going to try to keep him from doing what he loves.

After dinner, we were sitting around the campfire relaxing in the chairs we brought with us. Well, us females. The guys were ruffing it by sitting on logs. Augustas clapped his hands to get our attention, "So the nights' games are individual. We are playing two truths and a lie. This game will show how much we know about each other. The person that has the most points at the end of the night wins, two tickets to go see Taylor Swift in concert."

I looked at Augustas, "for real?"

"Um. No. You get a bottle of whiskey, to be used with Sunday night's game." And they complain about my drinking. Are they serious I mean they are giving away liquor as prizes this weekend? Of course, it has to be shared but still. We all took turns and so far no one was hitting on all cylinders, except Rosie and Augustas.

They were so sickening. I swear they were talking through a link. No one knew each other as much as they did. Rosie is my sister and I was tied with Augustas for being able to spot when she was skirting the truth.

When it was my turn I thought I would fool them and tell all truths. Rosie knows me so she should call me on it. "When I was five I tried to tie Rosie to the pole outside and Leave her there overnight but was caught by my dad. When I first came to school I had a huge crush on Marlo but never acted on it because I thought he was out of my league.

And I once ate an entire gallon of rainbow sherbet ice cream in one night. Everyone was guessing that the lie was my crush on Marlo, but Rosie knew I was telling the truth because she was the only one I told besides Danielle.

I looked at her and noticed she was sitting there thinking when she looked at me with the stink eye that was the moment I knew that she figured it out. Now would she call me out or would she bow out and not answer. I couldn't hold it in any longer I was laughing so hard I fell over, out my lawn chair. Rosie pointed at me, "you cheater."

Everyone was looking back and forth between me and Rosie. "What's going on?" Asked Bloom. I couldn't stop laughing.

So Rosie answered, "she told all three truths." She did try to tie me to the pole in the backyard when we were five because I wouldn't let her play with my favorite doll, and in freshman year right after we met you guys she had a crush on Marlo for about a month but he never paid her any attention so it left quick. And she did the ice cream thing last month after I made her a twenty dollar bet she couldn't do it." She pointed at me again, "cheater."

"Hey, only you knew they were all true, I was waiting on someone to pick something other than the Marlo story."

Marlo looked affronted, "yeah, why was it so hard to believe she would have a crush on me? I'm a great catch."

"Yes, you are," I said standing up. "Now I just look at you as an annoying little big brother."

"Aww, aren't you the cutest," he said pinching my cheek.

"Okay. Who's next since Rosie spoiled my answer?"

"You and Augustas are tied. So Rosie is going to say one thing and you have to guess if it's the truth or a lie." Stated Devon.

She put her hands on her hips. "Let me think. It has to be a good one. Last week while in my French class we were told to recite a poem and after I was done the guy sitting behind me told me I had a very sexy French voice."

Well, I'll be, that was a good one. If she is telling the truth Augustas will be skipping his Wednesday class and going to her class instead. I put my hands together behind my back and made a slow circle around her while giving her the side-eye.

"When this incident happened did you tell Theresa about it?"

"Yes." I flashed to Theresa to see her expression when Rosie said that. She gave away nothing. It was Augustas turn to ask a question.

"What did you reply back?"

"Thanks. I got a man." I had her. She would never say that.

Augustas looked a Rosie with squinty eyes, "you my dear are telling the truth."

"Wrong and right." Rosie knew I had her, she started smiling. "She is lying about what she said to him, but the story is true. Rosie under those kinds of situations would never respond at all. She does not enjoy confrontation of any kind. She probably thought to say that, it just never came out her mouth though.

However, I know the story is true because I remember walking in on her when she was telling Theresa I just didn't pay attention to what it was I just remember hearing in French class." And with that, I won. I couldn't help but laugh at Augustas as we were breaking up for a break. I heard Augustas whispering asking Rosie about the guy.

61

# CHAPTER 7

I went to bed early that night, if my memory is correct the drinking game night is wild, long, and too much fun. So I need to rest up for it, especially with the chores I have to do tomorrow. The next morning, or should I say crack of dawn, I woke to find the camp buzzing.

Bloom and Augustas were cooking breakfast over an open flame and grill. I spotted the girls over by the water and went to join them. "What are you three doing?"

Danielle looked at me, "what does it look like? We're washing up. Why aren't you washing up? Why do you look fresh?"

"Because my dear sisters, I'm smarter than the average bear. I have inside my tent a camping sink and behind my tent a camping shower. I have a water bottle that I put out last night next to the fire so that it got extremely hot and by this morning it was lukewarm and good enough to shower and brush my teeth with.

As long as you guys have been coming here I'm shocked you haven't done any shopping for camping supplies off Amazon." After I got done with my spill and looked at them they were staring at me with open mouths.

"You have got to be kidding me. We have been on I don't know how many trips and we never thought about getting those items. Well, this just blows. You bet your little knickers I'll have all and above next time. By the way how many showers do you get with your little water container?" Asked Theresa.

"I have two actually and after I got done doing everything I needed to do. I had used one and a half. I have an extra set. You three can pull straws since Kenneth didn't show I'll allow one of you to use his set."

They all started arguing about who should get the set, ignoring the drawing straws portion of my statement. "Whatever yall decide let me know tonight who I'm giving it to.

After breakfast, the agenda called for canoeing, the one sport that I truly did love and enjoy. Of course, it was set up where I would be in the canoe with Neko. We went up the river to a nice little spot next to a waterfall where we had a picnic lunch.

"Tomorrow we are going to do something we have never done before. If you don't want to go let me know now so I can take your name off the list." Announced Marlo.

By the smiles on the guys' faces, I'm expecting that they think us girls are going to bow out and leave it up to them to have all the fun. I don't think so. We are braver than they think we are. When I tuned back in I couldn't believe I heard my ears correctly.

"So what do you guys feel about that, should I leave your names down for the wild water white water rafting?" Are they out of their minds?

Braver than I felt, "What do you think, I ain't no punk. Leave my name down." I then looked at all the other girls, hoping I was not the only crazy person of the bunch. Blooms girl Freida, Devon's girl Lorraine and Marlo's girl Samantha all said they were coming.

Kamaray's girl, said no and so did Danielle with the comment, "I ain't dumber than I look." Theresa and Rosie, of course, said they were coming. This is either going to be the most fun I have ever had or I was going to die of a heart attack.

When we got back to camp I went to my tent to relax a little bit before we got on with the games tonight. Plus I had to leave in thirty minutes. I'm on fishing duty. The Fishing I don't mind.

63

It's the trek to the fishing spot that leaves me wishing for a different chore. After my two-hour fishing tour and coming up with three Fish. Neko had caught five Fish. When I arrived back to camp laughing at something Neko said I almost dropped my Fish.

"Hey babe, I thought I would surprise you and come on up for the last two days." Said Kenneth coming up to me and sticking out his hand to Neko, "Hey, I'm Kenneth Rosalyn's guy."

"Neko." He replied shaking Kenneth's hand. He took my Fish from me. "I'll get these to the guys so they can get them cleaned for dinner."

"Thanks. You came, for me? Thank you. You hate camping." I grabbed his hand. "Come on let me show you the tent and all the stuff I got so that it's not so bad." Another reason I wanted to get away so quickly is, that everyone was staring at us as if we were the show for the moment. Not.

He followed me to our tent. "Neko. Someone, you know?"

"Nope, apparently the guys didn't think you would come camping so they invited him so I wouldn't feel bad from having to sit out of team games. They wanted me to feel comfortable and want to come back again so they brought me a teammate."

He kissed me then hugged me, "well I'm here now so I can be your plus one."

"You came right on time too. Saturday is always the best night. It's the drinking game night and they always have some dumb game for us to play. This is going to be great having a partner that knows me. After lunch, we're going wild water rafting. Did you want to go?"

"Anytime spent with you Ros is great. Okay, so show me this stuff." And I did I showed him everything. His cot, sleeping bag, shower and sink kit, water holders for the shower, and the porta-potty. "Well that part of the tent, I said to him pointing at the makeshift bathroom, was going to be your room and I was going to set the bathroom up behind the tent.

But I didn't want to set up those two tents since you were not here. I changed your part into a bathroom with the shower tent being outside due to the water of course, but the sink is in this part which we can move outside if you would like or I can rearrange my side and we can share as long as you don't sleep naked."

"I can just share your space and no worries. I don't sleep naked."

I then proceeded to explain to him how to get hot water, then we went out back and hooked up his shower. I knew the girls were going to be so disappointed that neither of them would be getting the kit.

As we were walking from behind the tent he stopped me. "You know you are the best? You went way out to get everything I would need to be comfortable out here and being a butthead I almost didn't even show up. Will you forgive me for being that selfish?"

I gave him a kiss that should have knocked his socks off. "There is nothing to forgive, you're here now and that is what counts." When we made it to the fire dinner was complete and ready to eat. I asked Kenneth if he wanted me to make him a sandwich to go with the potatoes that were cooked for dinner. When Devon had to make a smart comment.

"Ohhhh, is Ken too sensitive to eat Fish with the rest of us?"

I rolled my eyes, "matter of fact he is since he would probably die since he is allergic to Fish." Devon sputtered out an apology in which Kenneth accepted in stride.

Later after dinner, while everyone was doing something to clean up Kenneth leaned in and whispered screamed to me. "None of them like me.

That is the main reason I don't come around or hang out in group activities. I hate being looked down upon without a person even getting to know me." While he was talking I was observing the looks of the others and they all looked ashamed and guilty.

"No worries babe I got your back. When we kick their butts in the couple's games they will be looking like judgmental losers." I said patting him on the cheek. Turning towards Augustas, "what time are we heading out to go rafting?"

"We leave in five minutes. Is Kenneth going?"

"Sure am. I wouldn't miss it for the world." We walked off towards the parking lot, we had to drive to the spot for the rafting, and since the parking lot isn't close to camp I headed out then.

⌻

When we arrived at the rapids it turned out to be an even lot with the girls that stayed behind. So, Neko wasn't left out to ride along with an instructor. I kind of worried about that, he did come all the way here to be my buddy for the weekend. I hoped he understands boyfriends come first, especially since I didn't invite him. The rafting was fun and scary at the same time. I haven't cried laugh so much in all my life.

66

One thing I can say about these guys they know how to have fun and give us girls and adventure. The funny part of it all was when Bloom's instructor got mad at him for almost tipping them over by standing up just to get his phone out his pocket to take pictures. Who tries to take pictures of near-death?

By the time we arrived back at the camp I was ready for a nap. However, I already knew that Saturday is our busy day. That's why I went to sleep early. No naps for me that would matter. Kenneth came up to me and hugged me from the back. "What are we all doing now?"

I took his hand. "Come, we're going for a walk before it all starts. Drinking games around here gets serious. I know you don't drink and that is fine if need be I'll drink for the both of us." I entwined my hand with his and walked off to the woods for our before walk game. "When we get back dinner should be done and then the fun begins."

When we returned to camp an hour later everyone was sitting around the fire, comments of about time, we didn't know how long you would make us wait. Did you need to take so long? It just went on and on. "Apologies, I lost track of time, we walked the trail up to the waterfall." They still gave me crap until I stuck my tongue out and gave them all the best finger I had, the middle one.

After grabbing Kenneth's chair and bringing it to the fire. I proudly announced that we were ready to kick some butt, bash some heads, take names, leave them crying in the dirt. "Umm sweets, are we doing something that is physically harmful? I don't think I would be comfortable participating in something like that. Interjected Kenneth. " I started laughing. "No, ha, I'm being overly dramatic, no physical violence."

"That's good to know. So what are we doing?"

Theresa jumped up, "we're playing the easiest game known to mankind ... Charades ... So with that, you all can bring it, because I know for a fact that Ros can't act out anything. Ha." The joke was on them. We were kicking their butt.

Even though I couldn't act out words that much when you spend as much time together as Kenneth and I do, and as much as we talk even though they think we just party, he knew what my dumb jesters and quirks meant.

Rosie sat back in her chair after my last turn, "Kenneth, I must apologize for thinking ill of you when it comes to my sister, any man that can read her like you do deserve to be with her, you have to pay too much attention to her to get this mess she's throwing out."

I couldn't do anything but laugh at that. Even though we were close in score Augustas and Rosie ended up winning. They should have since they're mated and should be able to detect what the other person is saying.

"That was so much fun. I forgot how much fun we have on these trips." I said stretching out on the lawn chair.

"That's the reason we always bugging you about coming with us, we miss you on these trips." Commented Bloom.

"Drinking game is next guys. So we will be using the bottle that Rosalyn won the first night." Handing Rosie the bottle they just won. "And that little gem will be used for the drinking game on Sunday." Announced Augustas.

"I interrupted what he was about to say next. I have an announcement. Due to personal reasons that shouldn't have to be explained, Kenneth doesn't drink so we have two choices. He could use water or juice, or I can take his drinks if he misses. Team choice."

"We don't want you to be a blubbering drunk, he can just use whatever he likes. That's cool with us." Replied Rosie.

Augustas proceeded to pour shots of the whiskey until the bottle was empty, he then took out another bottle for just in case. "The drinking game we will be playing is called sevens. I hope that you are all smart. How this works is we go in line starting with Bloom since he is at the beginning seat and going around the circle until it gets to me since I'm at the end.

Starting with one Bloom will start the count off, however when it gets to the person that will have to say seven or a number with seven in it you have to clap instead of saying the number. If you say the number you have to drink."

"If you have to drink three times then you're out and it's up to your partner to continue for the team. The last team or teammate standing that team wins. To make it harder we will not be starting off dry, everyone grab a shot and drink up. Also, after every twenty numbers we will all take a shot to make it harder and harder to focus."

The game was so much fun by the time we got to the hundreds it was a little difficult to remember what we were supposed to do. I was trying to stay focused on the counting, but it was getting harder and harder from the laughing. By the end it was Marlo against Augustas, they were going strong and we were sitting on the edge of our seat.

They were in the six hundreds. Shifter metabolism, crazy. When they got to the eight hundreds Augustas was done for and lost on eight hundred ninety-seven. We were all laughing and telling Marlo how good he did. As usual, the bag came out and Marlo's smile was not big enough.

The best part of winning the drinking games is the prize. There is a bag and in the bag are all the chores that we had to do at the camp, fishing, cleaning the fish, cooking breakfast, or lunch, or dinner, washing the dishes after said meal. Putting out the campfire and carrying the equipment back to the car.

Whatever he pulled is the chore he wouldn't have to do the rest of our stay here. That was the best prize that was always given out on the drinking games. The best part about it besides getting out of doing an unwanted chore, if you pulled your chore that was set for you to do the next day. You could give it to someone else and then you would have nothing to do.

Marlo had breakfast duty and he hated having to get up extra early to make sure it was done by the time everyone got up. Unfortunately, he pulled fish cleaning which was kind of cool since he hated doing that too. His girl pulled cleaning dinner dishes.

She was happy because that was her Sunday chore. She looked around and I knew the moment she had decided who to give it to. "I give my chore to Freida." She announced.

If looks could kill then at this moment Samantha would be a goner, because one of the rules of these games is you cannot under any circumstance pass the chore or not do it, If you do you will be blocked from playing any future games if you don't abide by the rules of the group. So Bloom couldn't save her this time manicure and all.

The rest of the night went off with us laughing and talking about different things. The main thing I enjoyed was how much everyone got along with Kenneth. It was kind of surreal, I was happy yet at the same time, I wasn't.

I knew within my heart that Kenneth was just for school and this would not go past that. No matter how much I enjoyed him and his company, I would rather he go out in the world and see if he can find or meet his mate. To settle for anything less would not be fair to him.

By Sunday afternoon I had released so much energy from laughing that I couldn't believe it myself. I didn't remember the last time I had this much fun with everyone. I was glad I came. As usual, we didn't do anything on Sundays since it would be winding downtime for us to leave the crack of dawn Monday morning so we could make our first eight a.m. class. Nothing happened during the day for me just sitting around the fire and toasting marshmallows.

Later in the evening and after my daily chore I had dinner cooking duties which were cool. I chose burgers, hotdogs, and bags of chips, which was nothing to sneeze at since the guys got three burgers and two hotdogs a piece. Us girls were much easier we only wanted one of each.

That evening we played our last night drinking game of keep going. There was a bowl full of sheets of paper with different subjects on them. We would pull the paper and if is said dogs, we would go in turn and name a breed of dog.
Whoever missed drank, as usual, we started with a shot but since we had an early morning we did not drink other than if we missed, and we only used one bottle once gone we were done. It was a fun night.

Monday morning came too fast, and when it was time to get up I didn't know if I wanted to kill Rosie for waking me and risk Augustas ire or just suck it up and get moving. I chose the latter. she is my sister after-all.

After stretching I looked over at Kenneth to see that he was already up. This weekend told me a lot about him. Regardless of the time, we went to sleep he was up before the sun even thought to peek over the horizon.

After leaving the tent I went to the fire to find a grand slam of a breakfast and Kenneth cooking. "I got up early and went to the store so I could cook a thank you breakfast, "here," he said handing me a plate with bacon, sausage, eggs, hash browns, and a croissant on it.

"Thanks, babe, you're the best." When I took my seat I noticed that everyone was stuffing their faces and commenting on how good it was. After a beat, Kenneth sat next to me with his plate. I looked over at him, "thanks again for this, it was very nice of you."

He smiled back at me "no probs."

After breakfast we all cleaned up, packed up, and headed out. Of course, I rode back with Kenneth and when he dropped me off we made plans to meet for lunch. We had our first class together and then after that, I wouldn't see him again for the rest of the day unless I meet him for lunch.

By the end of the day, I had just thought to turn my phone back on. Letting me know how much I didn't need a cell phone since I never even thought about it past getting it back from Augustas.

# CHAPTER 8

When I booted my phone back up I had maybe thirty texts come in from Gavin asking me where the heck I was at and why I didn't come to training this weekend. He must have thought I was joking when I told him I was going away for the weekend and couldn't get out of it unless I wanted my sister to find out what I was doing on my Saturdays. And I texted him as much and reminded him of the no cell phone rule and that I just got my cell phone back today.

He texted me back informing me that if I didn't come to training that evening for my upcoming fight this Saturday then I should find a new trainer because he only work with serious people, and blah blah blah, he went on with some other stuff. If he wasn't such a good trainer and person I would dump him quick.

After lunch with Kenneth.  When I showed up at the gym it was if Gavin had a GPS unit attached to my butt. He was waiting at the door with his arms crossed over his chest. I gave him a sheepish smile with a two-finger wave.

"Don't give me that, you wasted an entire weekend. I need you to give me fifty hands and feet on the punching bag, three sets of fifty pushups, three sets of thirty on the ten pound, twenty pounds, then forty-pound weights. You have an hour, then after that meet me in the ring.

Three hours later I thought I would just die right on the spot. If I assumed the level of Gavin's frustration with me, I downplayed it by a thousand. He worked me and when I complained I was dying he worked me more, and when I grinned and bore it hoping he would light up he worked me more, and the entire time with a smirk on his lips. By the time he was done with me, he told me he will see me at the same time on Wednesday.

When I arrived back in the room I had enough time to shower, write my report for my sociology class, and crash. Over the next few days, I trained, studied, and contemplated killing Gavin in a slow and calculated way.

He was able to find muscles that weren't even there, to work and condition. I fight Saturday and you would think that on Friday he would've let up, but he didn't, he went even harder at me.

When I was leaving he said a statement that made me realize his brutality of my past week training. "See you on Saturday at the warehouse. Hopefully, you won't lose this one like you did weekend before last." All I could do was look at him as he walked away. He knew about my fight, well nothing to do for it now, I've already been punished.

The night of my fight I tried my best to avoid any and all from the group so I wouldn't have to decline any plans or make up a consolation excuse as to why I didn't want to attend. However, I was not going to have such luck.

While I was in my room trying to gather my clothes together that I was going to change in at the fight. I was interrupted by my sister. "You gathering clothes, lets me know that my soon to be invitation to join us for dinner is going to be turned down."

I looked up as I was stuffing the clothes in my backpack, "yeah sis, maybe another time. I'll do something with you guys next Saturday." Since that is a no fight weekend I should be able to hang with them as long as I do training on Friday. Gavin shouldn't have any complaints.

"So where are you going?" I just looked at her and zipped up my bag. As I passed her to leave my room she grabbed the strap of my bag. "You're not going to answer my question?"

"Since you are my sister and not my mother I figured it was rhetorical, and up for my preview if I wanted to answer or not. I choose not. Enjoy your Saturday. I'll."

"That's it. We're so secretive now that you can't even tell me where you and Kenneth are going? Well, don't that beat all. I guess it must be some party that us peons are unable to attend."

I snatched my bag out of her hand, "and here I thought after the camping trip we were done being judgmental of Kenneth. But you were just faking the funk." She started to reply, I cut her off. "Don't bother. You will never like him, or trust him, or want me going out with him. So how about I don't bring him up and neither do you ever again. Deal?" Again I didn't let her answer. "Good." And with that, I walked out of the dorm room.

Who in the heck does she think she is? I mean I'm a grown woman. If I want to spend the night with a guy that is my prerogative. What beat all is the fact that I'm not even going to be with Kenneth, she just assumed and attacked him verbally. This is not what my mind should be on when headed to a fight. I need to be focused and concentrating on my opponent in the ring not the one outside the ring.

When I got to the warehouse I went off to do the usual routine of checking in, then I went to find Gavin. I found him talking to a guy that looked as if he had just walked out of a board meeting and came straight here. As I arrived at the duo, Gavin turned to me, "just the girl we were talking about. Rosalyn this is Mr. Jeffery Cummings, he is here because he is looking for the next female MMA fighter to take to the next level and I was telling him about you."

I was shocked but pretended not to be. I stuck out my hand, "nice to meet you."

He shook my hand excitedly, "Gavin has told me so much about you and I'm anticipating watching your fight tonight."

75

I smiled at him, "I hope I don't disappoint then." When it was time for my match the person that I was fighting was so far out my league. I wondered if Gavin had set this up. How many times am I going to fight someone that is over five-ten and look like they can bench press a car?

I went into my fight with frustration. Frustration for having to be constantly tested in these fights, frustrated with my life, and having to fight my sister at every turn, frustrated with not being able to say hey I do cage fighting, come watch me. I approached this fight differently than I had done before, I didn't care about her fighting stance, I just cared about beating her.

After the bell, I went in with full force. My very first move was to jump up and roundhouse kick her in the head which I saw surprised and dazed her at the same time. I didn't stop there. I used her dizzy state to sweep her legs and bring a palm to her chin knocking her head back. Then I did a twist curl on her arm, bringing it to an extremely uncomfortable angle getting some good points.

The rest of the fight did not go so easily. But I stayed on the defense. I also remembered what Gavin said about winning in round five and how that was a lost. With that in mind, I went hard like I did when I was training and by the third round, I had her pinned to the floor in a move that she could not get out of unless she wanted to break her neck to do so. I was proud of myself because I didn't even use my Fae strength.

After the match, I met with Gavin and the recruiter guy. He told me he will be reaching out once he was done with his recruiting tour. Gavin told me how proud he was of me and the fact that I got the tap out when I did.

Yeah, he was proud of me but not so proud that he didn't announce that he would be seeing me Monday at training. A girl can't get a break, even after a good fight. The life of fighter and trainer.

While I was waiting for my uber to show up I decided right then and there that I didn't want to deal with Rosie and her attitude so I was just going to get a room in town and stay there for the night. I text Kenneth to let him know so he would pick me up tomorrow. He said he wanted us to catch an early dinner before going to the party at the frat house.

I could only imagine that everyone was going to make an appearance since this was a party to celebrate the end of exams. Christmas break would be coming up around the corner and I'll be going home to spend some over needed time with the fam.

The next night while at dinner Kenneth asked me about the break that was coming up and rather or not I was going home and if not if I wanted to go skiing with his family. That was a shock to me since the first rule of our situationship was no meeting of each other's family since we were just having fun hanging while in college.

Good thing I was already going home that way I didn't have to worry about making up an excuse to turn him down. He is getting to close or is it my imagination. I shook my head to get the thought out.

"What time is the party? I wanted to stop at the store and grab me a new outfit to wear there. I don't want to wear what I have on now." I asked after telling him about going home.

"Oh, we have about an hour. We can run by a store. If you don't mind me getting dressed in your hotel room?"

"Of course not. It would be more efficient to do it that way, driving back and forth is a waste of time and gas."

When we arrived at the party the first thing I did was look around to see if I spotted the crew. They weren't there. Well not yet. I doubt they weren't going to come.

Kenneth and I were dancing and having fun when Rosie, Danielle, and Theresa walked in with the guys coming up behind. I noticed the moment she spotted me, I pretended that I didn't see her. Out the corner of my eye, I noticed that she was headed my way.

She stood just on the edge of the makeshift dance floor. Stop pretending you don't see me. You know I love you and only have your best interest at heart, even though I might show it in the wrong way.

I couldn't remember the last time we had used our link to talk to one another. When she first came through it shocked me. I love you too Rosie I just need you to mind your own business and let me live my life. You learn to do that and we will get along beautifully.

Your right. Augustas made me step in your shoes and asked me how would I feel if you were doing it to me and him. So I'm going to have a hands-off approach from now on. Just remember if you need to talk I'm always here for you. So are Theresa and Danielle.

I know Rosie and for that I'm grateful. Just wait for me to come for help and don't push it on me. You of all people know that when pushed I just push back. And with that, we were back in each other's good graces. I love my sister very much and don't know what I would do without my twin. I gave her a wink and proceeded to pay attention to Kenneth and us dancing.

After the song was over and we walked off the guys came up and spoke to Kenneth. It was nice to see them treat him like one of the guys. I even overheard them telling him about their holiday plans and wanted to know if he wanted to go with them. I enjoyed being able to spend time with everyone hanging out.

Monday after class I made my way to the gym to have my training session. "What are you going to do for the holidays? Are you planning on doing any training or fighting?" Gavin asked while holding the punching bag for me.

One more week of class and we will be headed home for some needed rest. I had to think about what I was going to do with the underground. I had to come up with a good reason as to why I have to come back early. I could miss one week of training if I get a day in all next week.

But two weeks and no fight. No can do. As long as I go home the family shouldn't complain. "I have to go home and see the family. But I'll only be gone a week. I'll leave right after Christmas and come back. To make up the lost time I'll be doing training every day this week."

"Make sure you do. You don't want to fall off as soon as a recruiter is looking at you for the pros." The pros. What if I did go pro? My family would have a heart attack. How in the world would I explain that to them? I'll need to focus on that when I come to that path.

Right now I need to book me a room in the nearest hotel so I won't have that far to travel for training, and that way no one will see me at the school. I just have to figure out how to get back here.

The perfect opportunity came to me while I was doing a shift at the hospital the next day. They were looking for someone to do a rotation either the first week or the second week of the break. I took the second week. And since it was from eight a.m. to one p.m. that still gave me time to get off and get some training in daily. Then on Saturday, I can have my fight after my shift. I'll just have Gavin request a late fight for me.

Man trying to have fun and live my life is exhausting. All this sideways planning and needing to come up with different ways to be able to do what I should be able to do without the aggravation. If everything works out then it will be coming to a head anyway. For me to go pro I'll have to tell everyone since the matches are televised, and I probably will have to quit at the hospital.

There is no way I'll have time for both. I'll have to make sure it does not affect my classes or my parents will never go with it. While I'm at home I'll have to figure out a way to bring up the possibility to my parents. But how? Something else I'll have to deal with when I get to that path.

The rest of the week was the same every day. Training, school exams, a rotation at the clinic, hanging with everyone at lunch, and when I say everyone that also included Kenneth. They were giving him a chance. Good for them and me. If we could all hang together it will make fight days and training days so much easier, no more splitting days, just one day of us all hanging together.

Except a couple of outings. Kenneth is wanting to spend more one on one time with me. I had the talk with him and he said it was not as deep as I was thinking, he just enjoys having someone to hang with outside his boys.

# CHAPTER 9

"Are you excited to be going home?" Asked Rosie. "I know I am. I don't know why this time it felt as if we were gone from home for a long time. I miss everyone like crazy."

"Yeah, I'm excited. I can't wait to see Jay. I miss him the most."

Rosie picked up her luggage, "come on let's go wait on the parental unit in front of the building."

Danielle and Theresa had already left. We could have driven home but our parents wanted to come and pick us up so that we could go Christmas shopping together before touching down at home. Which was fine with me since I have yet to get anyone a gift.

I picked up my luggage took another glance around to ensure everyone's room doors were closed. Closing and making sure the main door was locked I joined Rosie to go and wait out front.

On the ride home I hit my parents with the fact that I can only stay for a week. I made sure to make the need at the hospital worse than it was so they wouldn't say no to me coming back. It took about thirty minutes but they both agreed that doing the work that I'm doing is honorable. I agree. They didn't need to know the other things that were going to be happening.

When we arrived home everyone was there, my aunties were cooking a welcome home feast for the family. After hugging my aunts and uncles I went in search of the king of the family. Jay. He was the part of the family that was the best of us all, and you never knew what was going to come out of his mouth at any given time.

He was in the kitchen licking the bowl of a cake that I could smell was in the oven. "Hey Jay, did you miss me?"

"No. Why would I miss you?"

"Because I've been gone. I haven't been here in a few months."

"Don't see it. I play with my toys, go to school, and play with my friends. You old. I don't need to miss you. You can't play with me."

"I can play with you. What do you want to play?"

He shakes his head at me and grabs another finger full of cake batter. "Nothing. Don't you see I'm eating right now?"

"My apologies. Maybe later?" He rolled his eyes at me and turned back to his bowl of goodie. "Or not." Later after dinner, we all sat around discussing what we have been doing in school, or work, and how things are going on the farm. It was fun just sitting back laughing and talking with my family without the stresses of school or anything else.

The next morning when I arrived downstairs in my footie pj's I found my aunt and mother in the kitchen whispering something about the Fae elders and a letter that they received in the mail, about they are watching us. They must have heard me coming because they stopped talking.

I entered the kitchen. "Good morning family."

"Good morning." They both said at the same time.

"It should be a family census that if something is bad and it involves me and Rosie we should know about it." They looked at each other than towards me.

"It's nothing you need to worry over. Forget you ever heard anything," replied my mother.

I gave her my I don't think so look. "Mom?...Aunt Sasha?...Fine, that's the way it's going to be?" I grabbed a bowl, the Lucky Charms, and milk out the fridge and proceeded to fix me a bowl of cereal.

"What we should be talking about is the poor eating habits you have established since being away at school," Commented my aunt.

"Hey, they're in this kitchen so I'm not the only one with this eating habit."

"They're in the kitchen for when Jay stays over. You, my dear, should be eating real food." Stated my mother.

"If it's good enough for Jay, it's good enough for me." At that moment Rosie came into the kitchen and of course, I wouldn't be the sister, daughter, and niece that I'm if I didn't put my Mom and aunt on blast. "Good morning dear sister. You should know that these two are hiding secret letters about us, and the us I mean is you and me."

She looked at me then at the only two other people in the kitchen, "what secret letter?" she asked grabbing the box of cereal and fixing her a bowl also.

"You too with the cereal eating? And ignore your sister, as we told her the letter is nothing to bother with or give attention to," commented my Mom. She was so full of it. I could see the worry in her eyes as she was making her spill. I gave Rosie a look, and at the same time, she gave me one. We were on the same page. Find out what is going on one way or the other.

My mother continued making pancakes on the griddle and tried to casually throw in her next statement, "I think we should go out today so Rosie can practice her Telekinesis on big objects and human beings."

83

"What? Why in the world would she do that?"

"Yeah, I don't think I'll be doing anything of the sort. Just for argument sake, what human do you think I'll be flinging around the woods?"

"A dummy human, we have several set up with bricks in them weighing different pounds, from one hundred fifty pounds to three hundred pounds. So no worries with thinking you will be harming someone."

"That is all well and good. I still don't want to train or practice my skills. This is my vacation and I don't want to spend it practicing. Especially if I don't need it to protect myself. I'm safe at school. When I graduate and start traveling for my job I might need it in some hairy situations, but now. Nope." They looked at each other.

"If you say so, honey." My Mom might have agreed but she did not look like she wanted to in the least. After breakfast, Rosie and I took a walk to see the horses. At least that is what we told the parentals. When we got to the barn I looked behind me to make sure no one else was coming.

"You know we need to find that mysterious letter," I told Rosie.

"Yes. Do you remember when we were little and we accidentally found mom's stash of secrets, and we put them back and never told her that we had found them?"

"We strike tonight," I responded. "How are we going to do it. Someone would need to make sure she doesn't come to her room while the other goes for the letter. Said person then takes a picture of the letter put it back and we reconvene later in our old room to discuss. Now the question is who will be the brave one to go for the letter. I suggest we do rock, paper, scissors. The person in the room gets caught they might not outlive the repercussions."

As I was sneaking up the stairs to my parent's room. All I could imagine was my mother having my auntie glamour me to make me think I'm in my worst nightmare. I cannot believe I lost to Rosie. She knows I hate sneaking into our parents' room. I hated when we were ten and did it, I even hated it when we were twelve and did it because Rosie had to know if the secret stash was still there, and I hate it now.

I'm at the location. Do you have the subjects in sight? I asked her.

Yes, you are secure for operation retrieval.

I told you if I had to do this it's not called operation retrieval. It's called Rosie is going to regret it if I get in trouble.

Whatever just go for it.

And that is what I did. I went to the closet and lifted the floorboard that is under her favorite pair of stilettos, that she only wears maybe once a year. I found the letter, there was no return address on the envelope which made me feel as if I was barking up the right tree. I noticed that there were several more envelopes like the one we saw. I didn't have time to investigate them all. So I focused on this one.

Have it. Meet me in the room.

Since I was closer to the room. I made it before Rosie and it took all that was in me not to look at the letter before Rosie showed up. Matter of fact, since I'm that one that went into the danger zone I should read it anyway, I earned it. At that moment Rosie came into my room "if you've read it already I'm going to so dump your head in a bucket of water." She knows me so well.

"Of course I didn't do that." When she sat on the bed I pulled up the letter, and it read.

85

To the person that has cursed our nation with the birthing of twin abominations. You have been told that your daughters will be the destruction of our land and yet nothing has been done. Just know that we are watching your children and if the other one comes into her power.

Nothing will stop us from taking them out. We will not stand idly by while they destroy what we have built and what has been around for thousands of years. Watch yourselves because we are.

I just sat there. I reread it. "What are they talking about Rosie? Never mind you wouldn't know. I don't even know why I asked you, I'm not thinking straight, my mind is hazy after reading this."

I don't think Rosie heard a word I said anyway. "Rosalyn, I can't believe what we just read. This is why they wanted me to train today. Maybe I should take them up on it and catch some kind of training this week to be on the safe side."

"I think that's a good idea. We don't have much to worry about. I don't have any powers so we are safe from whoever wrote that letter. No worries Ro we will take this one step at a time, one day at a time."

"Yeah, your right. Thanks, sis for being here. Come on let's go bug Sapphire, you know how she hates when we crowd in her room. I need to do something to get that off my mind."

Rosie told my Mom and aunt that she had been unfair to them and if they wanted to treat her like a Ginny Pig then she was fine with that. So for three days now she has been going out in the woods with them after lunch and practicing maneuvers.

Of course, I have been tagging along to watch and give her a thumbs up when she does something good, and a thumbs down when she doesn't. It was funny and entertaining at the same time.

Before I knew it, it was time for me to head back to school. When I arrived and checked into my room. I went straight to the gym to get in a few hours. Working off all of the good cooking I enjoyed while I was home. Gavin also made sure to remind me every time I whined, about the recruiter that was coming back to see me fight again before he made his decision.

What would I do if he wants me? My family are going to freak out, my Mom is going to blow a gasket, and I might not live to sign the contract.

When Saturday came and it was time for my match I didn't understand the nervous feeling I was experiencing. After so many fights you would think I would be used to being announced and stared at.

I have had so many fights now that it should be second nature for me to get in the cage and do what I have to do. I went into my fight with one thing on my mind and one thing only. Impress the recruiter, get that pro contract, make that good money, and be happy.

And that is exactly what I did, I dominated in the ring, took my opponent out in the second round. I may be short, but I'm powerful and mighty. Gavin even commented that he noticed my confidence has grown and it shows in the ring.

After my fight, the recruiter told me that once I graduate from college, he will be looking to sign a three-year contract with me to fight pro. I didn't turn him down, and yet I didn't except. I have until graduation to give him an answer.

After my last fight and talking with the recruiter again this week. I decided that being the best at this sport and working towards the goal of going pro after I graduate is something that I'm willing to do. I know that my family loves me so they will grow to respect my choice in the matter.

Since school has started back up. I have been training religiously which means it has been a minute since I have hung out with anyone.

I know I couldn't keep telling Kenneth it was the crew wanting to do things and vice versa. Making plans with them and then canceling just to have an alibi is becoming exhausting. Sooner or later they will talk and my ability to keep doing what I'm doing will come to an end.

This weekend I have made plans with both. That should give me some freedom next weekend to return to my regular schedule. Tonight dinner and a movie with the crew. Tomorrow a party with Kenneth and then I should be in the clear.

I feel like I'm being pulled at all angles, and it's becoming exhausting. Something or someone is going to have to give. Funny thing is I know if I told Kenneth what I've been doing he would be down. I just want something that is mine.

The underground is a place that I can go and be myself without Rosie, Danielle, and Theresa looking at me with pity in their eyes. The defective Fae. In the ring, I'm all human, powerful, and in control. No one tells me what I can and cannot do in there. I mean there are rules, that's a given. But I don't have to hide my Fae side, I'm supposed to have some kind of strength to win.

# CHAPTER 10

Tonight, even though I should be fighting and going after that five hundred dollar prize I'll be putting on a good face and pretending to be happy to hang out with people that don't understand me, and act like they have to patronize me since I'll be the only single person there in the group. They try so hard to make me not feel like the last man out that it's exactly what they do instead. They try too hard.

Of course, the majority would pick a comedy. This is going to be harder than I thought it would be. Rosie knows I don't like stupid comedy where the acting is overdone, and punch lines are not funny, and the actors dumb acting is way past funny and have traveled into just bad.

Rosie gives me a look when the movie is picked, she knows how I feel about this. Theresa and Danielle are avoiding making eye contact. Let's get this over with. I can just catch up on my sleep while were here. I always give the couples their own space and sit separate, so when I do it now it won't seem strange. At least I thought.

Grabbing me by my arm, "Come on sis you will be sitting with us, we haven't seen you in so long, all that time you have been spending getting closer to Kenneth. Tell me is he the one that you are thinking about telling it all to?" Asked Rosie

"Nope, he is just someone cool I can hang with. He doesn't judge me or look at me as if he has these high expectations for me. We don't talk serious and we are not that serious, it's easy and the perfect relationship. I'm not looking for forever at this moment.

"I hear you on that," said Danielle.

Theresa grabbed my other arm, "there is only one thing I want to know. What kind of junk are we going to get?"

89

I couldn't help but laugh, "popcorn for sure, Jujus, nachos, and of course something to drink."

"Let's get going so we can stack up, and even better the guys are paying so the more the merrier," replied Rosie.

The movie was what I thought it would be. However the company was outstanding, I laughed harder at my friends then I did at the movie. Now we are at a pizza place eating. You would think we had an entire football team with us.

There are two tables pushed together the long way and six extra-large pizzas of different kinds, five orders of breadsticks, three salads, which the guys laughed at, and ten pitchers of something to drink down the center of the table.

The guys were pigging out like they had not eaten in years, even though they pigged out at the movies. I looked over at Rosie, "I don't know how they do it. Where does all the food go? Even for shifters, they shouldn't be able to eat their weight in food. I mean come on, just watching them is giving me a tummy ache.

"I know right. I tell Augustas that all the time. When we go on picnics I always pack two, one for him and one for us. I've never seen someone eat so much food."

"I'm glad I don't have to deal with that. Spencer being a Jackal shifter his appetite is quite normal. Even though he loves his meat he doesn't put it away like the rest of the group." Commented Theresa.

"Well Ricky is a wolf shifter and he doesn't eat as much as Kamaray. I think they take it to a whole new level," stated Danielle.

"Are you girls down there ragging on us and our eating habits yet again?" Augustas questioned. "Shifter hearing remember.

90

And here I thought you had so much love for me that you would be on my side, Ro?"

"Awww baby, you know I got your back. Girls stop talking about my big ole' teddy bear he can pig out all he wants to."

Augustas patted his stomach, "thank you. Now Bloom pass me a slice of that Hawaiian style." We all laughed at him. Rosie could only shake her head.

"You gotta love him."

After dinner I checked my watch, it was only ten o'clock which meant if I could get free in the next thirty minutes I could make at least one match. I just have to figure out how to get away from everyone, take the car, and not seem suspicious.

While we were walking to the car nothing came to mind. It looked like I would be taking an Uber, but it would be easier for me to take it from town. Which means I need to diss them now and not later.

"Well my peeps, it was fun hanging with you guys. I have enjoyed myself immensely, but I don't feel like going back to school just yet. I'm going to walk around a bit and window shop."

I knew the word shop would get them. Rosie hates when I shop and I know the guys would never be down for going from store to store, and by the look on their faces, my comment hit right where I wanted it to. I will have to peek in a few windows while waiting on my uber. This Fae no lying rule is exhausting at times.

Rosie gave me a look. "I would include myself in your plans, but I do hate shopping with you so I'll catch you later." She bent in to hug me and whispered in my ear. "You may have them fooled but I know you're not going shopping.

91

I can hear the slight falsehood of that statement, whatever it's your doing. Stop." It took everything in me not to react, I could not let her know that her assumptions were right. Who is she to give me orders.

I broke contact tapped her cheek and waved bye before walking off. Don't look back is the mantra I kept repeating in my head. If I looked back she would know I felt guilty. When I got to the corner as soon as I turned I put my back up against the wall and took a breath. It's impossible for her to know anything about what I'm doing.

I haven't been careless about covering up my bruises on my face with makeup, so I know she didn't find out. Think Rosalyn. Was there ever someone there that could have told one of the guys? Hmmm, I just don't know. Tonight I'll have to pay more attention to the crowd.

I learned a valuable lesson tonight, never go into the ring if your mind is not on the fight. I was so wrapped up in Rosie and what she said I couldn't get into the fight so of course, I lost. Matter of fact I got my butt handed to me.

One of the reasons was I couldn't stop looking out in the crowd to see if I saw a familiar face, in-which I didn't. I have to be overthinking this. Calm, that is the key when I get back to the school no matter what is said or done. I have to just stay calm.

When I arrived at the room, I had to take a moment before I entered. I shook off the nerves of the fight lost and walked into the common area. Who I found there is not the person I wanted to see after the night that I had. I went to the fridge to grab my sandwich I had put there the other night. I was starving after all the energy I used up in the ring.

However, it was not there. I moved everything around and couldn't find it. When I turned around I knew this night was not going to end well. "Please tell me, Samantha, that you did not take your slankie butt to this fridge and pull out a sandwich that didn't belong to you and proceed to eat it?"

"It didn't have a name on it." She sneered while still eating it in my face.

"Did. You. Buy. It?"

"Look it's no big deal, I'll get you another one okay?"

"I'm starving and I bet there might be one in the cafeteria, so I'll just wait right here while you run downstairs."

"Oh, I'm not going to get it tonight."

"Yes, you are. I want to eat my sandwich tonight. You stole and ate my sandwich tonight so you will be replacing it tonight."

She got up and tossed the remainder of my favorite Steak Sub in the trash, "I don't think so. It wasn't that good anyway. So, you can wait to get the trash sometime next week."

She went to walk out but I stepped in front of her. "I'm trying to be very patient. So I'm going to say this as calmly as possible. Samantha, I would appreciate it very much if you would go downstairs and replace my sandwich so I can eat."

She looked at me for a minute, just stood there looking at me. "Like I said. I don't think so." And she pushed me as to move me out of her way, but she used a little of her shifter strength because I moved. What she did not know is my strength as a Fae matched hers if not toppled it.

The next thing I knew, someone was screaming my name. "Rosalyn what are you doing? Stop you're going to kill her."

93

Theresa, Rosie, and Danielle were trying to pull me off, Samantha. When I looked down I was straddling Samantha and choking her, she was bloody. I couldn't believe I had blacked out like that.

Rosie got in my face, "Rosalyn are you alright? What has gotten into you?" You have not been the same lately."
I turned my back on her, "nothing is going on with me. She pushed me as if I was some weak human and I had to show her she messed with the wrong person. Next time she will be wary of putting her hands on a person."

Theresa shook her head, "no she won't. I'm going to heal her and wipe her memory of this incident, so you don't get expelled." And that is what she did. I was happy, but at the same time, I was disappointed that she wouldn't remember the beatdown I put on her. Plus I won't be getting my sandwich. Or maybe I will, just not tonight.

"Thanks, Resa."

Theresa touched Samantha's head.

"Memory come and memory go.
The memory of the day to fly away.
When you awake you will see.
That only asleep is where you've been."

Rosie looked at her and tilted her head. "Hey, no judgment that's all I could come up with at the last minute on the fly. Help me get her in bed you three. At least on top, I'm not dressing her in pj's."

"I'm going to go take a shower and go to bed. This night just blows." As I was leaving I heard Danielle asking Rosie what was wrong with me. That ticked me off. She could have just asked me. I just wasn't going to let it get to me, so I kept walking to my room. I didn't even care what Ro's answer was going to be.

94

The next night when I came out my room ready to go to the party with Kenneth I did into the stern face of my sister. Putting my hands on my hips. "Yes?"

"You're going out I see?"

"Yes."

"With Kenneth or by yourself."

"Not that it's any of your business since I never question you when you and Augustas go out, but yes I'm going to a party with Kenneth."

"Before you go we need to talk about what happened last night."

"There is nothing to talk about. Like I said, she chose to use her shifter strength against me because she assumed I was a weak human and got the surprise she deserved. Nothing more nothing less. Don't make more out of it than it is Ro."

She looked at me then looked back at the girls. "If you say that is all it was."

"Yes, that is it. If she wouldn't have put her hands on me first then it would have never happened. Bottom line."

"If you had something on your mind you wouldn't hide it from me would you? You would talk to me and not shut me out?"

"Of course. You're not only my sister you're my twin, and you two are sisters as well. If I needed to talk I would." See not a lie. Fae may not be able to lie but one thing for sure we can deflect very well. We are trained in the art of deflection, so we're not found out by someone asking the right question.

"Well, girls I have to get going. It's not like Kenneth can come up and grab me."

95

The party turned out not to be one that was being thrown by someone at school. This was off-campus and in a club. It was a friend of a friend Kenneth said. We were seated in the VIP section, which was kinda nice. As I sat back relaxing enjoying the music.

I spotted one of the girls that I had fought at the club. She looked at me and I gave her a look and turned my head hoping she got the message. I guess she didn't.

Kenneth leaned over, "do you know that girl over there?" I looked up and yes she was still staring at me.

"Nope," I said shaking my head. "I guess she doesn't like me sitting in VIP or she wants who I'm here with. I should be asking you if you know her."

"Naw, I don't know her."

I stood and leaned down and whispered in Kenneth's ear, "I'm going to go to the restroom, can you order me a Gin and Tonic with a Lime twist?"

Grabbing my face and giving me a kiss that would knock anyone off their feet. I knew it was a show to let me know he didn't know the girl. Which I already knew. "Sure doll, don't be gone too long."

"I won't." Walking to the bathroom, I did it in a way to make sure the woman would see me. And she did exactly what I thought she would do. She followed me. The thing about the underground fighting is I'm always fighting humans, so when they win they think they have done something supreme. This is one of those humans.

Not that she's not strong and a good fighter in her own right. She just couldn't stand up to my Fae strength if I chose to use it. I don't because I don't want any attention on me. I just want to fight and leave in peace. Seems that peace is going to be tested tonight.

As soon as I entered the bathroom I swung around and took two steps back giving her enough space to come in without giving her my back. "What do you want? I'm here with my guy trying to enjoy myself."

"Your guy? I never took you for the kind to consort with drug dealers."

"Well first off you don't know me to assume what I would do. And secondly, you didn't answer my question. What do you want? Because you didn't follow me to the bathroom to call my character into question."

"I'm assuming by the way you were ignoring me out there that your boyfriend doesn't know you are involved in the underground." I started to say something, but she raised her hands and cut me off. "I don't care either way. I'm not here to bust your balls, that's why I didn't approach you out there. But I need you to introduce me to him."

Has this chick lost her damn mind, "Let me get this straight You expect me to introduce you, a complete stranger to my guy, and why would I do something like that?"

"I want in on what he got going on. I want him to introduce me to his boss. I fight in the underground because I need the money. But if I could get in good with his boss then I could quit."

Before I could answer she pulled out a piece of paper, "don't say no. Here is my number, think about it and then give me a call if you agree to help me out."

"Why are you trying to get in with a low-level weed dealer? It can't be that much money in selling weed?"

She gave me a very strange look, "Huh."

"Huh, what?" But before she could answer the bathroom door burst open and Kenneth came rushing in grabbing me by my hand. "We have to go. NOW!"

I allowed him to pull me out of the bathroom. While running alongside him I couldn't help but look at the dance floor where a crowd of people was gathered around. "What is going on?"

"Don't know and don't care. What I do know is I'll never stick around anywhere to be questioned by the police. So we out of here."

On the way out the door, I looked back and saw the girl staring in our direction. Man was she desperate or what. When we got outside, we started walking casually and I heard a few tidbits from others talking.

Apparently, some guy had passed out in the middle of the dance floor foaming at the mouth. That sounded like an overdose to me, I have seen enough at the hospital to recognize the signs just by verbiage.

On the drive home I didn't even think about the girl until Kenneth brought it up. "I thought you didn't know that girl? But you were in the bathroom talking to her."

"I was not talking to her because I wanted to. She approached me about you. She saw me with you and figured since I was a female and close to you she could get in good with me so I would introduce her to you and you to your boss, so she could start making some real money, her words not mine. But I don't know her and I'm not vouching for her at all....I never knew the weed business was so lucrative."

"What's her name?"

"Huh, crazy I never got it. She did give me a piece of paper with her number on it to call if I chose to do her this favor." I pulled the paper out the pocket I had stuffed it in while being dragged out of the club. "Her name is Valarie. Also if I'm not mistaken she's human, at least I didn't sense or smell shifter on her."

"Okay, give me her number. Once I check her out and she clears, I'll give her a call."

I looked at his hand, then the piece of paper. I know he is not supposed to be my forever guy but giving him another chicks number is rubbing me the wrong way. I don't like it at all.

He must have seen the look on my face, he reached over and squeezed my thigh, "Hey, no worries. I'm a one-woman man. I don't want anyone else but you, were having fun so why go and mess that up with messiness? Trust me it's just you."

"Better be." Then I did something that I had a feeling deep down inside I would regret. I just didn't know why. I handed him the paper. What I didn't know at the moment was when it was all said and done Valarie's body would be found in a dumpster in Delaware.

CD

I was thinking about telling Kenneth about the underground club. He made a comment and I knew he was feeling as if there is someone else. The worst that could happen is he freaks out and tells my sister or tries to demand I stop doing it. But after all this time he will have to realize that will not happen.

He might want to join me and that would not be good to me, this is my time, my freedom, if he joins in he will take that away. I wouldn't be able to tell him that though he wouldn't understand.
I enjoy my time fighting I don't want to share it.

99

What if I just cut everyone out of my life? Then I could just do what I want to do without explanation. I'll think it over after my fight tonight. I have moved up two classes I'm the surprise that no one expected. Little old me getting in a cage and kicking major butt.

When I arrived at the club it was crowded and when I mean crowded I mean there were far more people here than I have ever seen at any of my fights. It looked like all the classes were here. I couldn't understand why until I saw the lineup.

Going across the board I saw my name and on the other side of my name was one name that I should never in my life ever see next to mine. 'Death'." I stood there for a while wondering who had lost their mind.

There was no way I was going to fight Death a gorilla shifter. I stormed up to Joe and stepped in front of everyone. "I NEED TO TALK TO YOU. NOW!" I pulled him to the side. "What in the world do you think you are doing? There is no way I'm fighting Death, are you crazy she is a shifter, top of her class, and double my height."

"Look doll. Let me be straight with you. You were a wild card when you came here, no one expected you to be any good or go as far as you went. We have no one else for you to fight. You can walk away and not fight this fight. Or you can take the fight not worry about the buy-in and earn yourself ten thousand dollars if you win and five thousand if you lose.

We have talked to Death and she promised to not use her shifter strength in the ring. You have an hour to make the decision. Enjoy the other matches. If you agree. Sign this release form and hand it to me, just make sure you do before the beginning of the last match."

100

I walked to the bleachers and took my usual seat. I have been coming here for so long that my name is on the wall behind me. All know this is not a place for them to sit. I have never sat at the bottom with the rest of the fighters. I always had to be to myself before my fights. It felt kind of surreal sitting here tonight.

And just think I was going to bring Kenneth into my secret life when this just might be my last night fighting ever. I should walk away. I know I should walk away. The money is not something to sneeze at though. That kind of money just to get in the ring.

This is the time where I wish my sister was here. I had to laugh at that. If my sister was aware of this I wouldn't be here. She would have totally snitched to the folks by now. Okay, okay, I have to think this out.

If I take the fight I'll have to use my Fae strength to survive, since she is way bigger than me and a shifter it will be fair. If I don't take this fight I'll never be able to show my face here again or go pro.

I could go at this like my third fight when I blanked out and dominated. I just need to get into that mindset again. I had made up my mind. I signed the form before I changed it again and headed to the back. I wanted to just be alone with myself. This will be it for me, win or lose this will be my last fight here.

When it was my turn, I was a ball of nerves. I think I made a mistake. I should have walked away. I didn't have anything to prove and I shouldn't have let Joe make me think I did. As I was walking up to the cage it was pandemonium. There were so many bets going on.

I wondered how many of them were betting I would lose versus win. For the first time since starting this, I realized I'm nothing but a spectacle to these people, a way for their income to increase. When I entered the cage, Death was already inside.

101

"You must be the dumbest human in the universe. Even if I don't use my shifter strength I'm going to wipe the floor with you. I'll take it easy on you and give them a show. But you won't be making it past the first round."

Now that just pissed me off. When she looked at me I know what she saw, a short, weak human. Well, I'm going to show her. When the match started I started off slow. I have seen her fight so many times but being in the fight with her it's different. My height worked for me when it came to her fighting style. Because she was used to tall people her low kicks weren't that hard so they didn't hurt.

The same with her swings. She had to adjust so much with the height difference that when she would bend down to attack I would use that and kick her good and hard upside her head. At first, I didn't use full strength but I wasn't fazing her. She was shaking off my hits like I was a butterfly tapping her. By the end of the first round, I was over this.

The second round I went hard, and I could sense her getting frustrated. She thought I was going to be an easy win, so making it to the second round I could see she didn't appreciate or like it one bit. By the end of the second round, I could see when her no shifter strength rule went out the window. She hit me so hard I felt like I was hit by a truck. Full Fae it is then.

When the third round started, she was in full shifter mode, and being Fae I could tell. She didn't know I could tell because she thought I was human. And the fact that she would go full shifter mode without shifting on a human-made me feel okay to do what I was about to do.

Time to take the gloves off with her. I stepped up to her and I was ready. I saw when the swing came and at the same time, I was throwing my punch as well. I knew at this moment it would depend on who made it first.

"Did anyone get the license plate of that truck that hit me?" Trying to focus and trying to figure out where I was, was harder than I thought it should be. I was even hallucinating that Kenneth was here. I closed my eyes back closed to give myself a moment.

"Babe, please tell me that you are alright because I can't holler at you for doing this if you're not alright."

"Kenneth, you are here?" I tried sitting up and couldn't. "Where am I?"

"You're in the back babe. When I saw you go down after that beast hit you, I rushed inside the cage and carried you out of there and brought you to the back."

"So I lost?"

"We don't know. I don't know if you had a brick in your glove but she went down when you went down, I just didn't stick around long enough to see if she got up. I honestly didn't care."

"How did you get here Kenneth? How did you know I was here?"

"I didn't know you were here."

"A friend of mine told me about this place and asked if I wanted to tag along and see this huge fight that was going to happen tonight. Imagine my surprise when this huge fight involved my lady. I want to tell you how upset I am with you but your hurting and I can't bring myself to do it. Yet."

"I'm ready to sit up. Not get up but sit up." When I sat up and looked around I could see that I was in a part of the warehouse I had never been in before, some type of infirmary beyond the one I had to visit a few times. Kenneth passed me a cup of water and I drank it slow. After collecting my winnings from Joe.

103

Kenneth told me that he would be driving me back to school. Since he rode with his friend to get here he didn't have to worry about it. We had a forty-minute drive that I knew was not going to be done in silence. And he didn't even wait for us to get out of the woods.

"You could have told me you know? I wouldn't have judged you or tried to stop you. You could have had someone there to watch your back. I can't believe you got in the ring with that shifter. Was it worth it?"

"To be honest with you Kenneth. Yes, it was worth it to me. I know it was dumb, but I had to prove something to myself. And no worries because it was my last fight. I had already made up my mind that if I did go along with that fight it was going to be the final one.

That fight was the product of them saying they had no one else in my class that I could fight, so I had to move over to the other league and they started with the hardest to see if I could hang. It was dumb to allow myself to be used like that. I know. I just wanted to shut them up."

"I can understand that people look at you and underestimate you because of your size. What made you get into this?"

"I just wanted something that was my own, something that was outside of my sisters and friends, and even you. I wanted something I could have all to myself. I found it in this."

"If I ask you a question will you answer it honestly?"

"Sure." If only he knew.

"How did you hit her so hard? How did you accomplish putting her on her back with your punch?"

"I knew that I had to put all my power behind that punch. I have been lifting weights and working out like crazy. I've been going to the gym and sparring with a guy so that when I hit a girl she would feel it. I'm happy I did too or she probably would have hurt me more than she did. Plus the rule was she couldn't utilize her shifter abilities."

"I'm glad you did too." He grabbed my hand and we rode like that to the school. "Are you sure you don't want me to take you to the hospital?"

"Yeah, I'm sure. I'm just going to go up and hop in the shower to wash away the day and I'll see you later on. Okay?"

He kissed me hard as if his life depended on it, "Okay. I'm sorry you lost."

"No worries. I didn't even expect to last as long as I did while in the cage with her. I lost but in my mind, I won."

# CHAPTER 11

The next morning when I woke up. I wanted to forget about my fight so I focused on the guy that had passed out at the club earlier that night. I went down to the cafeteria to see what news or gossip I could hear about what happened. Since there were so many college kids there it surprised me there was no news on the guy.

How is that possible? How could someone die and it's not all over the campus? Maybe due to privacy rules or something. Still surprising saying all the kids that were at the party. I hope the frat doesn't get in trouble since it was their party.

I decided to text Kenneth to see if he heard anything. He didn't reply which I found quite funny since he usually never ignores my text. It's Sunday so I know he's not in class, he should be texting me back. Also after last night, you would think it would be important for him to see what I wanted. I was just finishing up my food when I got a soft peck on my cheek.

I looked up to find Kenneth sitting. Straddling the seat while sitting his tray on the table. "Thought I would find you here when I saw your text after getting out the shower."

I just looked at him. "You couldn't text me back?"

"I figured why text when I can just show up."

"If I wouldn't have been here?"

"Then I would have texted you, chill babe. What's up with you, we have fun, so why are you busting my balls?"
"I don't mean to what you call it? Bust your balls. I'm just going to go on my little ole' way and leave you and your inconsiderate ways right here. Later." As I was getting up he lightly grabbed my hand.

"My bad okay. Look, I'm wound up with what happened yesterday. I apologize for not texting you back. I know you already ate, just sit with me while I finish my food. Cool?"

"Alright." I sat there. We did a little small talk nothing major while he was eating. When he was almost finished. I hit him with my question. "Did you hear anything about the guy?"

"What guy?"

"The guy at the club earlier last night. The party we ran out of. What did he overdose on?"

"Funny thing, well not funny but it seems as if it never happened. No one is saying anything, not even the people that I know were at the party. I didn't come right out and ask them, yet still."

"Yeah, I know what you mean. It's weird to me. But since we left I'm going to keep our presence there to myself. I don't want to be questioned by the police or anyone else for that matter."

Kenneth stood and picked up his tray. "Sounds good to me. I know you had a night and probably want to just go back to bed and sleep in. However, if by chance you don't, would you be up to catching a movie with me? I could use a change of atmosphere."

"That sounds good."

After the movie I returned to my room to lay down and rest, I was up quite early this morning and I also needed more time to myself. I thought about going to the gym but working out was such a distant thought I couldn't bring myself to do it. I thought about texting Kenneth to see what he was doing, but honestly, I just didn't want to be bothered. After laying there for a minute.

I decided to go for a walk and ended up in the library. While I was sitting in the library I overheard two kids talking about a kid that had overdosed, and even though it may be in bad taste I thought to myself finally. However, they were not talking about my guy, because the kid they were talking about OD'd in the gym. I also heard them mention steroids.

If I don't know anything I know the kid at the party didn't die from steroids. How much junk is being pushed on this campus? While I was walking back from the library I was thinking that it may be best if I stayed away from parties for a while at least until things calmed down. The last thing I need is to be mixed up with a drug scandal my parents would kill me on the spot.

And it's confirmed when I cross the Quad and see police questioning students. Yeah, not my animals not my zoo. I skirt around all that to head to my dorm. But with no luck, because as soon as I step inside I see they're in here also asking questions.

Seems I can't avoid it. Which sucks since I don't like having to talk to the police but tonight I'll have to. Hopefully, they don't ask me about any parties. Just my luck the only question they had for me was if I have heard of anyone selling steroids on campus.

That was an easy answer. That was it. Afterwards, I went up to my room. Maybe the kid at the party did die of steroids and that is why we haven't heard anything. Kenneth should be happy about that, so I decided to text him.

*: Hey Kenneth, the police just questioned me. It had nothing to do with the party, they asked me if I knew anyone that was selling steroids on campus.*

*: What did you tell them?*

*: What are you talking about? What do you think I told them? Do I know anyone that is selling steroids on campus?*

: No.

: Okay then. I just wanted to tell you they're on campus lurking around. Hit me up later on tomorrow if you want to get together for lunch.

: Cool.

When I made it up to the room the girls were already back. I hugged my sister as I entered the room since she was the closest to the door. "Hey, did you have fun camping.

"Yes. I did wish you were there with us. You were missed. Kamaray asked about you, he said it wasn't the same without you."

"Rosie, do you remember our last camping trip he had his tongue so far down his girl's throat the entire weekend I doubt he even noticed I was there. So I doubt it was any different this go-round."

She laughed, "You're telling the truth. The entire weekend we had to keep getting their attention for them to answer a simple question." I couldn't help but laugh.

I looked over at Danielle, "How was Ricky? Did he enjoy the cold, and ice Fishing?"

"You know he didn't, he does not like the cold at all, he and Spencer decided to spend the weekend either bundled up with me and Theresa or sitting by the fire drinking cocoa to stay warm and trying to complain as less as possible. We even had to pull rank. They were even talking about renting the cabin a few miles down. Go figure, big ole shifters freaking out about the cold."

I thought about it for a moment, "if you think about it they are not Bear shifters with fur to keep them warm, and even Bears Hibernate."

"I'm just glad we convinced them to see it through this weekend. We had to make a deal with them." Replied Theresa.

"What deal was that?"

"We would go to a hockey game with them next weekend and this would be the last ice Fishing trip we force them to go on," grumbled Danielle.

"Oooo Wee, you two hate hockey. They must have been miserable to the highest power for you two to agree to that."

Theresa shook her head, "yeah they were. We felt bad for them."

Rosie jumped up off the couch, "I had one too many smores this weekend, I think I'll head over to the gym and get in about an hour's worth of exercise. Either of you girls want to join me?"

I shook my head, "not me I think I'll be busy doing the lunge-crunch exercise."

She stopped in place and looked at me, "what is that?"

"Lunch, I'm hungry plus you know I don't do exercise, catch you three later."

"Nope. Wait up I'll go with." Responded Danielle.

As we were walking down the hall Danielle bumped her shoulder with mine, "I've missed you lately, we don't hang out like we used to."

"I know, I know. I promise things will change, it's just you know how it is, when you and Ricky were new we barely saw you, just give me the benefit of the doubt. I haven't left you all, just finding my way."

She gave me a quick sideways hug, "I understand Ros, truly." I just smiled. The rest of the trip to the cafeteria was done in silence. While we were eating Danielle had me laughing with the telling of all the antics that the guys got up to while they were gone.

By the end of her tale, I was sad that I didn't join them. I told her about the steroid overdose. I didn't tell her about the party. I just couldn't take the chance of being hassled.

The next night after class I had a shift at the hospital in town. When I arrived it was booming with patients. I was informed by the charge nurse that they have had to pump the stomach of three shifters and two humans, and they have also had four overdoses in this one night.

The police have been scrambling all day trying to figure out what is going on. When I inquired if they were all college kids, she told me that they were not. Only one human stomach pumping and one shifter stomach pumping were from the college.

The rest were from the town or the town one over. Sadly, people died. However, since it was not all college kids, that let me know it's someone off-campus that's doing this horrible thing. Too bad there's no way I can find out any information to help the police.

For a few days now I have been going through a conundrum I know if I get involved I'll regret it, I also know there is no way after Sophomore year the crew will be up to doing anything else that could get us tangled up in a web of crime, we almost died and came close to having to expose ourselves.

111

I would like to find out what is going on but not at the sake of my family and friends.

To keep my mind busy and off the things going on here I decided to just dive into my studies. Unfortunately, that meant not spending as much time as I would have liked with Kenneth, it sucked but on the weekends he only wanted to go to parties. I didn't understand his obsession with college parties.

Rosie, Danielle, and Theresa seem more laid back since I have been spending more time with them on the weekends instead of going off partying. I still feel like the extra man out when they couple up and go places. Kenneth is never available when I ask, or he refuses to be available. I'm not sweating it though. He is not my forever guy.

I wanted to be out there partying with him, to be honest. Since I wasn't fighting anymore my weekends had become mundane. After that big last fight with 'Death', I turned down going pro. The possibility of exposure was too high.

I figured after the couple of weeks that I spent with the crew Rosie would get off my back and I can get back to hanging with Kenneth. I don't understand how she doesn't see that partying is a righteous part of college life.

After a couple of weeks, I started back with my party life. I just had to do it with more of a sneaky nature. When they asked me to do things I made sure to have other things to do that I can use as an excuse like going to the library to study or going to the gym. I hated doing that, but a girl got to do what a girl got to do if she wants to have any sort of social life.

I mean not everyone can be a goody-two-shoes like my sister and her best friend. And Danielle is so wrapped up in her personal life she doesn't have time to monitor mine.

While I was in la-la-land my phone dinged with a call. "Hello."

"Hey babe, I was wondering if you wanted to go out of town with me this weekend?" Responded Kenneth on the other end.

"Out of town with you where? And I hope this is not a plow to try to get into my pants, because like I said unless you putting a ring on my finger that's not happening."

"Whoa, slow down with the wedding talk. Make a guy get hives. No, I already know where you stand with that, and like I told you if and when I'm ready for that next step you will know. To answer your question I have to go out of town for a function at my boss's house and since you are currently my lady I figured it would be cool to have you on my arm." My smile was huge when I heard this. "I also don't want to ride alone, and George can't go." And there the smile went.

"Even though it sounds like I'm your second choice after George, I'm still going to go just to use you as a means to get away from the school for a weekend." Ha, two can play that game. "What time are we leaving? I'll have to pack a small bag. Also is this little function dress up or casual dress?"

"We'll be leaving in two hours, and as far as clothing just the normal stuff you wear will do. The night of the function you will need a cocktail dress. I know you have a thousand of those in your closet. Grab one, something bright and cheery."

"Cool, I know what to bring. I'll see you in two hours. Text me when you're downstairs. Oh and so Rosie won't send out the national guard. Where are we going exactly?"

"Oh yeah, we'll be driving over to Delaware. Not that far."

"That's cool. Make sure you get snacks for the road."

"Cool." And with that, he hung up. That man is frustrating more times than not.

When Kenneth arrived to pick me up I was about to explode. He didn't tell me that even though George was not going, Zeke was, and he knows I don't like being around Zeke. He does not respect boundaries, his jokes are crude, and he chain smokes Marijuana like he is afraid of not being high.

I keep telling Kenneth he is one blunt away from rehab. Kenneth thinks I overreact since Zeke has been on the Dean's list since we started school. At least that is what the rumor is.

Kenneth must have noticed the look on my face. "No worries babe, he promised not to smoke in the car." I was not convinced he could go that long. I looked at him and got in the back seat. I told Kenneth I would rather sit in the back that way I have the entire seat to myself and can lay across it when I want to sleep. The truth of it I just don't want Zeke at my back. Something about him just rubs me the wrong way.

Zeke turned his head to face me. "Yeah no worries short stuff, I can withstand smoking, you shouldn't listen to rumors and judge a person by them you know."

I wanted to first punch Kenneth in the head for repeating what I talk to him about, and then two punch him again for discussing me with Zeke at all. "I don't just listen to rumors, and I don't judge people. I know for a fact that you chain smoke since I have seen it with my own two eyes. By the way, the rumors that I told Kenneth about in private." I said snarkily. "Was about you being a jerk and not knowing how to treat females. And by the crude jokes that you tell I would say I believe it."

His eyes bugged out, "What are you talking about, girls like those jokes."

"No. We don't. They are nasty, defacing, and downright not funny."

"He turned back around. Women."

This is going to be the longest weekend in the history of weekends. Breathe Ros Breathe. I have to do my meditation technique before I punch him with the strength I don't suppose to have. I gave Kenneth a death glare in the rearview mirror and he dared to wink.

Awfully long weekend. I decided at the first stop to get gas that I was going to make the best of it and just go along without causing trouble, and since Zeke didn't light up not one time it made it easier.

Leaning against the car as Kenneth filled up I thought to make small talk. "So what is your boss's name? I don't want to go in here unaware."

"Pent."

"Pent, who names their kid Pent?"

"His name is Pentium, but he hates that hippy name, his words not mine, so he calls himself Pent, and anyone that wants to keep their job does also."

"Cool, I can understand that. He should have it legally changed. So what does he do for a living?"

"First, he didn't change it because in wolf shifter culture when you're giving a name it's for a spiritual reason so you must keep that name. It has something to do about our name being given from the Lords of old. Anyway. He deals in antiques. He searches for them and then ships them all over the country. That is what I do for him delivery within the states. He says why pay the full shipping price when he can have people deliver."

"That's smart I guess. I'm going to go to the restroom before we head out." While in the restroom I wondered why Kenneth would deal weed if he had a job doing deliveries for this guy on the side. I thought about asking him. I just really didn't care enough to find out so by the time I got back to the car I had let it go.

# CHAPTER 12

When we arrived at the house, well that is an understatement. What we were standing in front of was nothing less than a mini-mansion if I had to name it. It was huge. "How many rooms are in this place?"

"I don't know, I do know that there are ten bedrooms. Five in the west wing and five in the east wing. I have never had a real tour. Never felt the need to. Since we will be here all weekend you might just get the chance."

I bobbed my head up and down, "I never really asked, why are we staying the entire weekend? The party is tonight right? Why not leave in the morning?"

"That's easy, we have some business to go over. Pent thought this would be a good chance for us to take care of two birds with one stone."

"Hmmm. Wait, business, so that means you are going to leave me alone in this big house to fend for myself while you go off to do business with your boss?"

"Of course not, his lady will be here also and you two will keep each other company. Duh. I would never do that to you, babe."

Well, I'll be, this man drives me all the way here to spend time with not him, but a complete stranger. At this moment I wished I was a witch so I could turn him into a toad. That would be funny a wolf shifter toad.

I went to get my bag out of the trunk when I noticed he had already grabbed it. Oh yeah, he carrying my small bag. He knows I'm not happy. It's going to take more than him to carry my bag to make up for this little incident.

117

When we entered the house I was even more amazed. I don't think I have ever seen such elegance in my life, I felt as if I should be putting on those hospital shoes the surgeons put on their shoes when going into surgery just to walk across the floor.

I think I'm in the wrong business. Walking in the house the open foyer area with tall indoor trees cut thin in the corner.

I love the double-sided stairway going up to another part of the house, and to not be confused, the sign at the bottom that says west wing east wing tells you what stairway to use.

Looking towards the room to the right I can see that it's the dining area, the table that is in there looks like it can sit at least thirty people. The room on the left is the ballroom with the most gorgeous crystal chandelier I have ever seen.

The host and hostess were the human versions of Ken and Barbie. I thought I was seeing things. I wanted to ask Kenneth if they were who the dolls were made up of. Pent had Blonde hair, blue eyes, and muscles on top of muscles. While she was a Blonde, slim with long legs. They were both tall, and here I'm standing a full 5'4'. A weekend of looking up, oh goody.

"Aren't you just the littlest thing ever. I'm Gracie and I was told that you would be my weekend buddy while the guys do what guys do."

"Hi, I'm Rosalyn, it's nice to meet you."

"Come on with me girlfriend, let me show you where you'll be staying. You will be on the west wing with me and Scooter," Scooter? I knew it. Ken and Barbie. "The guys will be on the east side, so no worrying about man snoring." When I blanked out I thought I heard her say something about this being a fun weekend. I hope. Plastering on the best smile I could muster, "I can't wait."

Later that night I expected Kenneth to come and get me from my room to take me downstairs to the party, but Gracie had a different idea. She was in their prompt and early with her hairstylist to do my hair. It was such fun laying back being pampered like that.

Like I said this is going to be a great weekend. Especially since she is a woman after my own heart. Tomorrow we will be going shopping I was told, who doesn't love shopping?

When I arrived downstairs I was amazed at the transformation, decorations were hanging all in the foyer, Kenneth was waiting at the bottom of the stairs and by the look on his face, I knew I did well. "You're beautiful babe."

"Thank you. You clean up nice yourself."

When we entered the ballroom or dancehall whatever they call it. It was also decorated beautifully. The atmosphere was relaxing. Kenneth kissed my knuckles to get my attention, "You want something to drink?"

"Yeah, a glass of champagne is good thanks."

"Okay, I'll be right back." While standing there awaiting Kenneth's return I gazed around the room.

"Would you like to dance?" When I looked up I was staring into the eyes of the most handsome man I have ever seen.

"Excuse me? I asked if you would do me the pleasure of this dance."

"Oh, that's nice, however, I'm here with someone he just went to get me a drink."

"So that means you can't dance? I'm B-.

"Bret, it's so not good to see you here tonight. I see you've met my lady, Ros. If you'll excuse us we were just going to find us a seat." With that, Kenneth took me by my hand and after handing me my drink and walked off. Well shucky now if dominance wasn't on display at that moment I don't know what was.

"Who was that?"

"That my dear is the competition. He has been after my position for a year now and we just don't see eye to eye at all."

"Got it, stand clear." The rest of the night went off without a hitch, except for the times that Bret would find his way somewhere near me whenever Kenneth was called away by Pent or stepped away for some other reason. I can honestly say that the attention was nice but unwelcomed. Future or not I'm a one guy girl. Outside of that, I don't think I have danced so much in my entire life.

"Hey love, would you like to take a walk outside in the garden before we turn in?"

"I would love to." The garden was beautiful, being Fae we appreciate flowers and this garden has several different kinds and the smell is amazing, makes you appreciate life. "It's so beautiful and welcoming out here," I said spinning around in a circle.

"Yes it is and so are you. Thank you so much for coming with me this weekend, it meant a lot to me."

"Your welcome." I don't think I finished my reply before he was kissing me. I don't know how long we stayed like that, but it was quite amazing. When we finally broke apart I couldn't help but smile.

Kenneth grabbed my hand, "I think we should go back in. We both have an early morning and I can bet that Gracie is not the one to be kept waiting."

Kenneth wasn't wrong, who gets up at the crack of dawn to go shopping? Gracie that's who. I could have used like three more hours. I guess she reckons shopping is an all-day event. Pent had a car for us to go wherever Gracie's little heart desired. His words, not mine.

"I figured we would go shoe shopping first." I looked at Gracie, who was enjoying a small cocktail in the back of the town car we were in.

"Sounds good to me."

Now I'm not the type of person that would complain about shopping, and if you asked my sister Rosie I'm a shopaholic. However, there is a shopaholic and then there is a person that needs shopping anonymously.

I have never seen someone find so many things to buy. We went to every store known to man.  By the time we were done, I was exhausted and was on the verge of swearing off shopping for a lifetime.

Well, maybe not a lifetime but at least a month, thinking it might be better for it to be a week. It also never hurt to shop with a person like Gracie who insisted on paying for everything that she picked out for me, that I picked out for myself, and things that I was trying to be adamant about not needing.

We left at nine in the morning and didn't return until after three. I told Gracie I needed a nap when we finally did get back. She said she understood and will have my things brought to my room. She called it a room, I called it a mini apartment.

It was huge. Living room area, bathroom suite, and then a bedroom with a California King bed. Climbing in under the Down comforter that was on the bed, felt like bliss. Before I knew it I was in la-la land.

What awoke me was a knock on the door. "Coming." When I opened the door is was Kenneth standing there.

"I figured you wouldn't want to miss dinner since you already missed lunch." I knew I was tired but not tired enough to sleep until dinner.

"Thanks, give me a minute to brush my teeth and freshen up."

"Cool, I don't mind waiting."

"My apologies, come on in and have a seat."

While Kenneth made himself comfortable I went into the bathroom to do what I needed. "What time are we leaving tomorrow?" I hollered out.
"Around noon."

"Cool." Stepping out of the bathroom. "I'm ready."

We headed downstairs to the dining hall where there were about twenty people already seated. I whispered to Kenneth as we entered. "Is these employees or house guest?"

"Mostly employees. Their good peeps so no worries." The night went smoothly, great conversations, good company, and a sweet guy by my side. What more could a girl ask for? After dinner, the menfolk had business to discuss, so Gracie took that time to pull me into the game room to watch housewives of something or another. I wasn't paying attention. I have never really been a reality television watcher.

"Hey! Since my show is over do you want to go to the lounge and have a nightcap?"

Lounge? What doesn't this house have? "What lounge and where?"
"It's in the basement. Scooter likes his toys." When we got to the basement it was huge. It was an open floor plan. With a small kitchen, bar, movie theatre, bathroom, and a half-open door. When I went towards the door the scene was out of a movie.

A man was sitting in a chair and I could have sworn that Pent knuckles were bleeding. As I got closer that guy Bret noticed me and closed the door. Weird, I can't say that he was beating the guy but it sure did look iffy from my short time view. I might ask Kenneth about it later.

We were seated at the bar having ourselves a drink when the door finally opened. Out came Pent, Kenneth, Zeke, Bret, and two other guys I have never seen before. One of which looked like he had seen better days. But he was walking and talking on his own accord, so I guess what went down was no big deal. That made me feel better. No need to question Kenneth. I didn't think the antiquing business was so severe.

Everyone joined us at the bar except for the two guys I didn't know. We laughed, talked, and drank some good expensive brandy. Even though he seemed to be too serious about his business Pent was a nice guy. He was laid back and very welcoming. I went to bed early that night. I wanted to make sure I was well-rested when we hit the road.

Overall this was a great weekend. Before we left Gracie made sure that I took her number so if I'm ever this way again I can hit her up, and if she's ever in Vermont she will make sure to reach out to me. After everything was said and done, I liked Gracie.

When we were leaving I couldn't help but put a smile on my face. "Kenneth, I must say thank you for this weekend, I enjoyed it immensely."

"Anytime love, anytime."

The drive back was uneventful. Zeke was even quiet. I wonder if something had happened, he is never quiet. Yet it's not my business so I'll not be asking him. I enjoyed myself at least. After an hour I couldn't take it anymore. "Zeke I know I'm going to regret this, but what's up?

I mean you would be chattering nonstop to the point that I want to strangle you. We've been in the car for an hour and you have not said one word, or attempted to strike up, with me having to remind you I like my air clean."

"Oh, Ummm, to be honest, I have a bunch of stuff on my mind. I need to work out what my next move is going to be. I was given the possibility of a somewhat promotion by the boss. I need to weigh the pros and cons of taking it."

Kenneth looked over at Zeke, "I didn't think it was optional."

I looked back and forth between the two, "How is taking a promotion not optional? How can someone force a person to take something they don't want?"

"Our boss is different, when we first started working there we had to sign a form of agreement as to the length of time we would be employed, and that in that time we will take any promotion given to us as long as it doesn't affect our school time." Replied Kenneth.

"Man, that's some serious job." The trip home was quiet, and I slept more than I was awake, by the time we made it back to the school I was ready to be out of the car. I kissed Kenneth and told him I would hit him up later and made a mad dash to my room.

124

When I got there I busted inside and I singsonged "I'm baaack." There was no answer, that sucks. I guess they must be out with their guys. Go figure. Guess I'll change and go grab some food in the downstairs lunchroom.

I thought about just fighting in the underground again and just not going pro. It didn't' work out. After that last fight, and all the damage that I took I decided it was in my best interest to leave the fighting alone. Especially since Joe would not guarantee me that the same situation wouldn't happen again.

Even when I told him that there is no way to guarantee they won't use their shifter side. Because I could guarantee a few times 'Death' hit me with slighted shifter hit. He just shrugged his shoulder and with that, I knew I was out. Gavin wasn't too happy about my decision and chose to ignore my calls and text as a way to show me.

So, I was back to my partying ways. I thought it would be much safer and smarter if I didn't get outed by having any more fights with shifters. Kenneth and I have been going strong partying every weekend with the disappointed view of my sisters. I would have thought that after all this time they would have lightened up just a little bit.

Kenneth, on the other hand, was happy. He told me that even though he would have had my back, he feels so much better that I'm not putting myself in such harm's way. If only he knew. Tonight we were headed to a Rave. I have never been to one so I was excited at seeing how they go.

After doing much research on the internet. I had my backpack with me, inside were two bottles of water, an extra pair of comfortable shoes, earplugs, two bandana's, extra pair of sunglasses, a short roll of toilet paper, and an extra set of comfortable clothes.

125

Kenneth also had a backpack and a cooler. When I asked him what was in the cooler. He informed me that is was beer and Wine coolers for me. A bottle of Martel and cups. He said I should never under any circumstances accept a drink from anyone. And if I happen to want to buy something make sure it's bottled and pay close attention to the fact that it wasn't opened.

When he saw the look on my face he squeezed my hand, "it's fine love. Although many individuals will be there to have fun, there are sickos wherever you go and many of them love to roofie females and you will not be one of them. Other than that enjoy the music and we will party hard.

I have us sleeping bags and non-perishables, the rave is due to last all three days so we won't be leaving until Sunday. There are five bands playing tonight, four different DJ's tomorrow, and Sunday will be ended with Marshmello. David Guetta. And Martin Garrix. So we will be having a great time this weekend."

When we arrived and parked Kenneth pulled out the supplies and handed me a couple of bags to carry, the cooler was on rollers so that was good because it was huge. He had two backpacks, not one. "We have a long walk until we get to the Rave. Also Pent set up a food truck for us here. If you get hungry for some real food then eat at the truck that says, 'Food for Foodies' only."

"Is he here also?" I asked.

"Who Pent?" I nodded my head yes, "no he wouldn't be caught dead at one of these, but he understands his employees needs to relax and unwind, and since he puts so much training and money into us, he makes sure to protect us even from ourselves at things like this. Therefore the food truck."

"Well, that's nice of him." When we arrived at the entrance. I was shocked to see that it cost us fifty dollars each to get in. Good thing Kenneth paid or he would've been upset with me when I asked him to take me home. I only pay that much for my clothes and shoes.

The music was lively and people were plenty when we entered inside. There was a band playing hard rock and you could tell the rockers, by the way, they were jumping around and banging into each other. I tried to stay on Kenneth's heels as to not get lost in the crowd.

"Ros, look around, where would you like to set up at? The Front closer to the stage, middle, or in the back somewhere you can hear the music but we can also hear each other talk?" I chose between the middle and rear, we could still hear each other but we were in the midst of others that have set up camp.

Three more couples showed up that worked with Kenneth's company. I was happy for that, not to be here alone, and to have other females to talk with this weekend. Kenneth spent most of his time walking around. Me I lounged around on the blanket enjoying the music.

Good times but I was glad when Sunday came. When the weekend was over and we returned to school it was to the disappointed vocals of my sister questioning me about where I've been and why I didn't answer my phone all weekend. How she acted you would've thought I was a child or at least her child. The argument we had that day was worse than any we have ever had. I was getting fed up.

# CHAPTER 13

The week went past with me and Rosie not speaking to each other. I decided to get away for the weekend and go visit the family. While I was there, my Mom took me to a rehab place to volunteer and see what happens to people with addictions. I could only guess why she would do that, it had to be in honor of my sister and her big mouth about my partying lifestyle.

It did give me a wakeup call, there are more young people in rehab in Vermont than adults. And since I'm more human than Fae reminds my Mom, I need to be careful since we do not know to what extent I can tolerate things going into my body.

I wanted to smart off and tell her that I was not an alcoholic and I knew what I was doing. But I knew how far that would get me, so I just stood there and took every lecture. I was required by my mother to volunteer at the center for three days a week whenever I came home.

Graduation is not going to come fast enough so I can get away from everyone and they can live their lives, and I can live mine. It's exhausting trying to live up to everyone else's expectations of you.

While I was on my trip Kenneth called me every opportunity that he could, the last time I spoke with him we promised to meet up for lunch once I got back to school. I'm back and I'm anticipating seeing him soon. I need to talk to him and let him know that partying Rosalyn is no longer here. I need to do whatever it takes to keep my family off my back.

�

My first week back at school was supposed to be welcoming after all that I went through while I was at home. I thought my life couldn't get any more frustrating. I find myself looking into the face of the man I thought I would never see again.

128

I worked hard to avoid him and even harder trying to forget he even existed. I would have loved nothing more than to be with him if he wasn't human. I couldn't, wouldn't subject a human to the life of being with me.

Not only is he standing in front of me he is looking at me as if I have committed a cardinal sin. I know I didn't give him a reason for ghosting him when I did but it has been an entire year, you would think he has gotten over it. It's even funnier since I just dreamed of this same situation two nights ago, out of the blue I dream of him and then here he is.

I pretend to not know him, I'm on a date with my boyfriend Kenneth who's a wolf shifter, and in all my time of dating him I have never heard him speak anything concerning humans but with bad intent and the need to stay away from them. I don't know what is going on.
What I do know is that even if I want to avoid him, I have to make sure nothing happens to him when it comes to Kenneth. Wolf shifters are territorial, and they do not play nice.

"Let me do the introductions. Jordan this is my girl Rosalyn. Rosalyn this is my new roommate.

"Nice to meet you," I said nonchalantly. "Kenneth, are we finishing lunch? You know I have to get back."

"Sure, sure. Jordan did you need anything? I can meet you in the room later. My little lady here works at the hospital and is short on time. We must finish our lunch so she can get back."

"I'll see you over there. Nice meeting you." And with that, he turned and walked away.

"You too," I said quickly returning to my meal as to not give Kenneth any suspicion. I needed to hurry up and eat so I can get back to the hospital and have a mini breakdown.

129

I remember those eyes the color of the sun, and those long pupils that should've scared me only made me want him more.

When we hung out in my freshman year. I knew I was in trouble. I determined at a young age love was off-limits. I'd sworn to myself I would never love anyone. Love gave people power, and I knew at a young age that I'm the only one that will have power over my heart. That's why I dated Kenneth he was easy and simple. Someone I knew I didn't have to worry about it going any further than dating. With Jordan it was different.

⊕

I couldn't believe my eyes. The last time I saw her we were having lunch in the Quad freshman year having a good time. At least I thought so. After lunch, we went our separate ways with the understanding of seeing each other again. However, after that lunch, I never saw her again.

At one time I even thought that maybe I imagined her. We didn't run in the same crowds so I didn't see her on campus. She never answered any of my calls or text. She was just gone with no word at all. I thought we had a great time.

It took a lot for me to work through what she had done without any explanation. I guess the best thing that came out of it was, I was able to focus on the start of my career. Having no girl in my life gave me the ability to focus on this assignment. Having no one I was able to take this undercover gig for the local police department I applied to do my internship at.

It's finally coming close to being done. It has taken me two years to get this close to KJ and convince him that it would be in his best interest if he introduced me to the top boss that was supplying him with the drugs he was distributing on campus.

I never would have thought that the day I was to have my first meeting with his boss and needed a clear mind I would run into Rosalyn at the diner in town having lunch with a drug dealer.

130

I mean what is she doing sitting across the table from the man that will soon be in custody. First, what is she doing with the likes of him? Second is she involved? Will I have to arrest the woman I have been dreaming of for the past two years?

*Our mate is smarter than that, she would never be involved with the likes of a man like him.*

-She is not our mate, she left us without explanation. We're here to do a job. Nothing more, and if I have to arrest her you will do nothing to try to stop me.

*I won't have to do anything. Our mate is not a criminal and she definitely is not involved in drugs and money laundering.*

-I hope you're right. For now, we have a meeting to get to. The last thing we want is for KJ to get mad and cancel this.

*I doubt he will cancel, he's too money hunger for that. Greed will make sure he shows.*
-First, off its money-hungry, not hunger, and second I hope that you're right. I'm tired of having to room with him, he's such a pig. I'm ready for this to end.

KJ is a shifter and with that comes heightened senses. I need to pull myself together before this meeting. I don't want him to feel my hate for him, which is now intensified by the fact that he has who I want. When I walked into the building I made sure my mind was clear. I had a new focus. I would need to push forward without any apprehension.

KJ took me to his boss and I could have never imagined it would be Pent, Pent Reed, he attended the university and graduated three years ago.

131

"KJ here tells me that you are good with sales and retrieving money. He told me how you helped him out at a party when someone decided to not pay him for the items he provided to them. Seems to me and KJ that you're a good person to have around. So I'm going to give you a probation period, one week to show me what you got."

"What will that intel?"

"It will intel you bringing me five thousand dollars by the end of the week."

"Five thousand? And what if I can't obtain that much?"

"Then I would advise you. The day before the final day you should arrange your last rites. When I see you it will be the final stage. So it's in or out, no in-between. Now get out of my office sooner than later and don't return until Friday."

After meeting with Pent I had only one thing on my mind. Mr. Reed has to be the first person that I takedown in this organization. Leaving out I didn't know if I wanted to strangle KJ or tell the police that this was too much for me to handle. How in the world was I supposed to sell five thousand dollars' worth of drugs in one week? Matter of fact. I'm not selling drugs to people period. Looking over at KJ, "is he serious with that?"

"Very serious, and he must like you he gave me three days."

"Three days, how in the heck did you sell that much in three days?"

"I didn't. I had some money saved for a car that I didn't buy. I gave him that and so it began. I would get rid of his stuff, then sell mine until he gave me more. If I was ever short I would just use my own money. The crazy part is, the money I made was more than the money I had to put in, so I benefited at the end of it.

If you happen to have any funds lying around do the same thing, you will make twice your money and save your life. Whatever happens, in the end, don't say I didn't warn you about wanting to get into bed with Pent. He is not someone to mess with."

"I'll think about it, first thing first I'm going to try it the old fashioned way, I mean I have a week."

He handed me a duffle bag. "Well then in that case, here you go." When I opened the bag it was full of Opioids, Fentanyl, and Stairway. Stairway, that drug sounded familiar I just can't put my finger on it. I have to ask someone about that one. Which means doing something I just might later regret.

⊕

"I can't believe you're dealing with Kenneth if anyone would have asked me if your moral compass was that low I would argue them to my death that they didn't know what they were talking about."

"That's rich coming from the girl that is sleeping with the same person that you think I should steer clear of."
I looked at him with the eye dagger of death. "First off I'm not sleeping with anyone, secondly it's none of your business, third I date him because he is safe, I don't have to worry about catching unneeded feelings."

Raising his eyebrows. "Huh! So is that the reason you left me the way you did, avoiding unneeded feelings?"

This is not happening, not now not never. "If that is what you came to my job to talk about how about we don't. I have better things to do with my time then to recollect the actions of my freshman year."

133

He was standing there looking as if he was wrestling with himself. He looked like he was having a profoundly serious internal dialogue. I could see when he came to a decision, his face relaxed.

"My apologies, you're right. I'm working with KJ and I would like to know what I have in my possession." I gave him a nod to continue. Have you ever heard of Stairway? I know I heard it before I just can't grab onto it. You being in the medical field around different drugs and dating a known dealer I figured you could lead me in the right direction."

"What are you talking about? He deals in Medical Marijuana which if you haven't heard is legal. But concerning that drug Stairway, I've heard that name also. I'll need to seriously think about it to figure out from where."

"Rosalyn, I don't know what you are talking about. I just left a meeting with him and his boss I know for a fact that he is not dealing with Marijuana. Medical or any other kind." Looking at her I knew she was surprised at what I was saying.

I had to seriously look at him. "Are you being serious right now? That can't be true. I've been to the parties with him, a little recreation drug is all." I looked at him and he was shaking his head back and forth. "What drugs Jordan?"

I didn't know if I should involve her more in this since I was not just dealing with KJ. Pent is dangerous. "Rosalyn I didn't come here to get you involved in anything more than assisting me in finding out exactly what Stairway is, do you remember or not?"

Pulling out my phone I tapped a few keys looking up the information I thought would help me. Yep, there's the article that Augustas wrote. "That drug Stairway is a drug that a professor that worked here had developed for mind-controlling shifters.

134

We took him down and all of his research and work was supposed to be destroyed. How in the world is it still being reproduced? No need to answer it was rhetorical.

What are we going to do call the police on him? Or would that be calling the police on you too now that you're involved with this too? How could you deal drugs that could do so much harm? I would hate for you to go to jail. What do you expect me to do? Why did you put me in this position?"

"No need to worry about that Rosalyn I have it all under control."
I put my hands on my hips, "outside of calling the police on him and yourself. How do you have it under control."

"Is there somewhere we can go and talk in private?" I knew what I was doing was the craziest idea I have ever had. But if the rumors are true about what she and her crew did Sophomore year then she may be able to give me some insight.

I took him to what the interns and first years call the alleyway. It's a place that we go to study and complain about the residents. Since it's off the grid of traffic, quiet, and secluded. I didn't give him a second of entering the room before I was on him for answers. "We're here no one will disturb us." Looking at my watch. "We have a good twenty minutes before anyone comes back here to do any studying. So go. What do you have to tell me that is so secret?"

"I'm still in school as you know, and I'm taking criminal justice if you remember our conversations from long ago." The look she gave me told me to avoid yesteryear comments. "Anywho. I had an opportunity to advance my career by going undercover for the local police department to bring a stop to the drug problem that is happening on campus.

135

The police got me in the room with KJ and with the perfect staged encounter allowed me to get in good with him and get a certain job that will, as he thinks, help me with the opportunity for my family to overcome financial problems."

"What if this big boss searches your school records and sees what you are taking in school. I mean everyone knows criminal justice is either law enforcement or lawyer and I don't think he will care either way before disposing of you."

"I don't have to worry about that since this is a huge case the police are working with the FBI and my records have been forged to show that I'm into agriculture. I'm doing my part to take down KJ and Pent. Pent is the big boss that is running this area. Thanks for the information it was a great help. I need to run and check in to tell them about Pent and the meeting. I'll make sure to tell them about this drug and where it came from. Hopefully, they know how it got on the streets or was not taken off in the first place."

"I thank you for your thank you but I'm going to help with this, and before you give me any of your macho man stuff. If that drug the professor manufactured is on the streets then it involves me. I was a part of the original team that brought him down and was sworn to that the drug would no longer be a problem. Yet here it is a problem. At the end of this, WE should know where this drug is coming from."

"Something tells me that if I don't agree with you assisting me I'm going to find you sneaking around behind my back. I accept your help. But on my terms, and that's not negotiable. You are with me or I'll have the FBI put you in a safe house holding cell until it's over. And before you ask yes, I'm threatening you."

What could I say to that, his terms were cool since I wanted to see this to the end. "You got a deal." I stuck out my hand to shake on it, and when he touched me, the feeling I got caught my breath it was like a zing went through my body.

I pulled my hand back and pretended that nothing happened. If he doesn't mention it then I'll not be mentioning it.

I could tell he felt it too by the look on his face and the way he was holding his hand. "Again thanks for the information. I'll call you later when the time comes." Before I could reply he was out of the room and walking away. I knew it was for the best, nothing could come of this. We may have a connection, but he is still human.

# CHAPTER 14

Months of small jobs and doing what I'm told to do without question from this maggot KJ I finally get the break I want. Out of the blue, I get a call telling me to be at the pier at eight o'clock. This is part of the job, so I do it. This could be the big break to finally finish this.

⊕

I woke from my nap after having the weirdest dream I have ever had. I dreamed Jordan called me telling me about this job that he is being sent to do and he is going to use this shipment to bring them down. When he takes the shipment to the police department it's nothing but toys.

However, he was followed and when he shows up with the package to the people he working for he is killed. I woke up with a fright, it seemed too real, I could feel the shot that he received to the head.

When I went into the common area to get me a bottle of water out of the fridge when I got the weirdest text ever.

*: Hey Rosalyn, I have to do a job tonight. My very first shipment so this should be over sooner than later. I'll just turn it into the police when I'm done, then they can bust Pent. So thanks for the offer of helping but I won't need it after tonight.*

Looking at my watch I see that it was still early.

*: Jordan, I know you have no reason to listen to me, but whatever you are thinking don't do it, don't take the shipment to the police, it's not what you think it is. Take it to the warehouse like you're supposed to. I had a dream as weird as that sounds. Trust me this one time if you never trust me ever again.*

I didn't get a reply back. I hoped and prayed that he listened to me.

138

I was sitting in the car waiting for them to load the package into my trunk when I received a text from Ros. I started to ignore it but something about how she was talking made me think about it.

*Our mate is smart if she tells you to do something just do it.*

*-I think you are going a little too far, I'll listen to her to a certain extent, and it just so happens that this one time is one.*

*Whatever you say.*

After the shipment was loaded I went to the warehouse to drop it off. I was already flustered because I showed up twenty minutes before the scheduled time and they weren't here, the boat was an hour late. Another test probably to measure my patience level. Well, I've reached it.

When I arrived at the warehouse the big boss was there, he is always at every drop to make sure everything is what it's supposed to be. Months of working for this guy all I wanted to do was smash his face in and call it quits, but I couldn't.

Getting him on tape doing something illegal was the game plan. Getting out of the car he came over to me and clapped me on my back. I didn't understand what that was about until he spoke. "Looks like I was wrong about you.

I had you followed tonight, I just knew you were too good to be true and that something was up with you. KJ told me I was wrong, I'm glad he was right, killing you would have been a shame. Anyway, don't you want to see what you went to retrieve?"

When I went over to the table and he cut open the boxes I was shocked. Toys, nothing but miniature toys. I have to buy Rosalyn a gift because if I would have taken it to the police I would have blown everything for toys.

*Told you.*

*-Stuff it.*

"I'm glad you got your toys here safely. I have classes in the morning so I'm going to go now."

"Cool, cool. Now that I know for sure you are trustworthy the jobs will increase and so will the loads. You are someone I can see going far within this organization. You have a knack for it."

"Thanks." He would say I have a knack since I was able to give him the five thousand and on time. Good thing it was the FBI money because there was no way I was selling those drugs to my fellow classmates.

After I told the police where that drug Stairway came from and they looked into it, it seemed as if the good professor had a partner that Rosalyn and them didn't know about. So he was able to continue the process of manufacturing the drug.

The F.B.I. investigated and took him down, so now the FBI is the provider of the Stairway drug to this organization, which gives them another way in. The only difference is the drug is a copycat without the hallucinate property added to it.

Several jobs later and going to meeting after meeting. I was able to get to know Pent very well. I have been following his life for a year now. I know his routine better than anyone. I know that he golfs on Mondays, has secret meetings that he attends on Tuesdays and Thursdays.

I know that his business is a front for his money laundering because nothing is ever shipped in or out, I know he has never gotten his hands dirty yet he is responsible for the death of about five shifters that he has felt crossed him. He is evil plain and simple.

140

"Hello."

"Let me first say thank you for the text message concerning that shipment. I'm sorry I haven't been able to reach out to you before now but between Pent giving me all of these darn jobs, having so many meetings with him, classes, and trying to keep my head on straight I haven't had time for myself. You will never guess what was in that shipment.

"What?"

"Toys, nothing but toys.

That didn't surprise me since my dream. "Well, thanks for calling. I started to think you had lied to me at the hospital that night."

"Nope. Matter of fact to make it up to you. I have bugs that I need to get in place in his business and the warehouse. They need full proof evidence of his dealings that he could never dispute. The first part of the plan is already in place for his home.  The Maine police department will be putting bugs in. However, there is someone always at the warehouse and he spends more time at his business than he does at home. So putting bugs in there is going to be a task."

"I guess you need me to help put those bugs in?"

"Later after my meeting with him, I'll be hitting his warehouse and installing what I need. The hardest part will be his office since that is where he spends most of his time. I'll have to think hard on this, but it has to be done and soon. I really wanted to just plant the bug today at our meeting, but I have never been inside.
We always meet at the warehouse.  I don't know rather or not he does sweeps, the last thing I need is for the bug to be found after

141

I met with him. I'll have to choose wisely, when, and how to put it in."

"I know you probably don't want to involve more people, however, the one person that was able to get us inside the professors home was Marlo. His father owns a security business and Marlo works with him during his breaks. The one thing he taught him was how to get into anything, any place, anywhere, just in case he had to do a rescue. We could work together and come up with a plan to get inside."

"I don't know about that Rosalyn. Will he be able to keep it to himself and not tell the rest of your crew? This is dangerous for me, if it was to get out to KJ I could lose my life. I don't want to lose my life."

"I promise you Marlo can keep a secret. Just let me call him."

I was dubious with telling her it was okay. The only reason I did was I had no other way to get into the office. I certainly don't know how to break and enter. We decided to meet at the diner for her to make the call.

"I hate to bother you with this, but I need a favor and you have to keep it between just you and me. You can't tell Rosie. She would never understand what I'm doing or why.

"I'm still listening." Said Marlo.

"I need you to get me and Jordan into an office building  Then inside a certain office. I can't tell you exactly why just know that you will be helping to take down the person that is involved with Stairway."

"That's all I needed to hear. I'm in. Let me know when and I'm there."

"Thanks, Marlo. You're the best." After hanging up the phone I looked at Jordan. "He's in he said just tell him when and where."

"I have a meeting with Pent in his office. This is a first. He is trusting me more. After the meeting, I'll have the lay of the building. It's good too since I didn't know which office was his. We would've been going in blind and hoping to find it before we were discovered."

"Oh yeah with that plan Marlo would have killed you. Let me know when. I have to get going I have an afternoon class."

"Okay, talk to you later."

After leaving from Rosalyn feeling good about the prospect of getting the proof needed to get this thing ended I received a text from Pent. I assume it was him. He never uses his name just a time, date, and place. Of course, it would be tonight. At least I won't be going to the warehouse to drop this shipment off but to his office, so it has to be something irrelevant.

When I arrive at the drop off spot. I walk into his office to not only find Pent there but a room full of people. To my surprise, this is when he introduces me to the top people in his organization which confused me until he told them that he has been watching me and knows that I'm the person that he feels is right to be his right hand and to learn from him someday to take over the business. I smile the biggest smile I can muster, while thinking won't he be surprised at the end of all of this.

While at the meeting I hear him making plans to go out with his lady friend and thought this would be a great time to go into his house and see what I can find. Instead of trying to get in myself, I figured this would be a great test for Marlo to put my mind at ease.

143

*: Hey Rosalyn, do you think Marlo would be up for a test run tomorrow night? I want to go to his house tomorrow, he will be out with his girlfriend. I figured we stake out his house and go in as soon as he leaves.*

*: That sounds like a good plan. I'll text him and find out if he is available.*

I sat there drumming my fingers on the steering wheel waiting on her reply. I guess I should drive off before Pent looks out and wonders what I'm doing. Not that he could see me from the sixteenth floor. It's better to be careful than sorry.

The next night I parked my undercover vehicle, of course not the same one that I drive every day down the block from Pent's house. Sitting there I wished that it was just Rosalyn and me so I could have talked to her more on the private side. I guess just having her here is better than nothing at all.

"So Jordan. Where have you been all this time? I mean one minute you were around and then the next. Poof. Gone."

"I ended up getting so wrapped up in school and my career. I felt it was better if I fell back and stopped bothering Rosalyn."

"At no time did you bother me. My headspace when it comes to relationships is much different than anyone else. I didn't want to get too deep into a person when I needed to focus on the direction I wanted my life to go. You were the kind of person I could have lost myself in. Freshman year was not a good time to do something like that."

"So after this, will be seeing more of you?" Asked Marlo.

"I haven't really thought about it. But I don't think so. I have to keep my mind on my career and advancing in that. That takes up most of my time. Sleep and school take up the rest."
"I can understand that," replied Marlo.

144

When Pent finally left his house we exited the vehicle. "No one should be home at the moment. Hopefully, he will be gone long enough to give us time to get in look around and get out. I have this spray we can put on that will muster our scent, so even with his heightened senses he will not associate the scent with us."

*I like that you finally have the wolf scent, I have never liked that I'm a part of you and yet you do not carry my smell at all.*

*-I know. I have decided that after this I might just continue to wear the spray so that you feel recognized and wanted. Because you are wanted, and I want others to know that I'm a wolf shifter without having to explain it all the time.*

*Thank you, that would be very much appreciated.*

After we sprayed ourselves really good with Marlo complaining about how it was sacrilege to force a bear shifter to smell like a wolf just to do a job. Either Rosalyn or I owed him a steak dinner with dessert, at that awfully expensive steak house in the next town. Of course, Rosalyn volunteered me saying your mission your fee.

I scanned the street as we approached his house to make sure no guards were posted. It was secluded and dark, perfect for what I needed to do. Going around to the back would be too suspicious, I'll be going through the front and leaving out the back.

I learned from the crew that put in the bug that he was too smug to have an alarm system. I bet he thought. Who would be dumb enough to break into his house? Me. That's who.

I told Marlo and Rosalyn that after he does his deed maybe they should go back to the car. Of course, Rosalyn argued, but Marlo agreed when I told him I needed him to keep watch and if he saw anyone coming to call, not text, call Rosalyn. He agreed and went back to the car after letting us in.

145

"Gloves on," I told Rosalyn.

"Gloves on."

"We are looking for anything that will tell us that he is dealing drugs, buying drugs, or anything of the sort. They have not been able to get anything on the bug since he barely only sleeps and eats here. So I'm trying to find anything."

Rosalyn looked at me, "got it."

When I entered the house I was surprised at what I saw. It was dull and boring for someone with so much income. The tile on the floor was worn and missing in pieces. The house itself was as small as it looked on the outside. I see why he spent the majority of his time in his office. That is where he put all his money. Because this is a dump. Good thing it was only a one-floor one-bedroom house.

Which tells me this is not his main home. I hope that is not going to be a problem with proof. But I understand why they are not getting anything on their bugs. "Rosalyn come on. we need to move fast." And that is exactly what we did, we checked every nook of his home and as I thought there was nothing here. He has to have a second home and I'll need to find out if KJ knows where. "Let's get out of here there's nothing here."

Leaving that day I was quite discouraged. I was hoping my mood was brought up by any good news that KJ provided. I had to play it smart though, get information without him knowing I was seeking this information.

⊕

Hanging out in the room with KJ one night I took my chance. I knew that they would hear us over the bugs that I planted in the room. "KJ how much money do you think we can make long term doing this?" He looked over at me then rolled his eyes up as if he was thinking hard on my question.

146

"I would say in the millions if we are smart about it and invest our money."

"Seriously millions? I think you need to go lower, looking at the house that Pent lives in we're not going to be making millions."

He started laughing and shaking his head. "I never thought you were so dense, that dump isn't his house. I can't believe you would think he would live in something like that, have you seen his car, his office, the way he dresses.

Please, that dump is his house of confusion, that's what he calls it. It's the address he uses just in case someone is on to him and search info on him they will find that one. His real place is not even in this state or in his nickname.  It's in his middle name which no one knows."

"I only know that because he told me one night after a big job and I was talking about buying me a nice car.  That was my speech on how to survive the game by hiding what you don't want to be found. That's why he spends so much time in his office. There is a room off his office that he sleeps in. He only goes to that dump to throw off anyone that is following him."

"Well, that's smart. I hope one day I'm that smart since this is the profession I choose to dabble in."

"I hear you on that man, I hear you on that."

# CHAPTER 15

There is a big shipment coming in and I know after all this time it's the big one. I call in the heavy hitters so that they can be there to take them down. Rosalyn swears that she will see this to the end.

When we enter the warehouse KJ is there. He shouldn't be. When Rosalyn sees him she looks back and forth between us and plays it so cool she could have won a reward for her acting.

"Hello, Kenneth. Is this the reason you haven't had any time for me these past two months? Too busy selling drugs?"

"Naw. You got boring. You stopped partying, just wanting to do couple stuff. I couldn't make money sitting in a movie theatre or restaurant. Or on a stupid blanket in the park having a picnic. I had to do what I had to do. It was fun while it lasted but we both knew it wasn't going anywhere. It didn't take you long to move on I see.

I ignored that jab. "I'm glad you cut it off. You're a murderer."

"No, no, I'm not a murderer, but I'm a criminal."

"How could you say you not a murderer? People have overdosed and died from the crap you have sold to them."

"Rosalyn dear, if not me then the next man would get the money. Don't judge me when you're standing here with your new boy toy for the same reason I am."

I decided to interject before the conversation went somewhere I didn't want it to. "We're all criminals here so let's get this over with. What time are we going to get this shipment? I assume you're coming along since you're here? Even though that wasn't the original plan."

I asked KJ wondering if he would say something about Rosalyn being here and tagging along to pick up the package with me. Well ... Us now.

"In fifteen minutes they should be there. So we need to get going.

Well, let's get going. I'll drive, Kenneth you can sit in the passenger seat, Ros you in the back. Since neither of you knows where you're going."

What KJ didn't know was Rosalyn was bugged. She is trusted since Pent knows her through KJ It won't be weird seeing her here when we drop the package back off. But she will be able to get the entire deal on tape. One thing I do wonder about is the purpose behind the change and sending KJ with me.

"The plan if you don't know it KJ is to go to the pier pick up the package drop it off back here to the big guys with all the money and then we leave. Go to the party that is being held tonight and get our party on. You good with the partying part Rosalyn?"

"Yes, very much so."

The part of the plan that KJ doesn't have any idea about. Is the police will be there at the warehouse, set up and in position to take everyone down when we get back.

⟋⟍

Pent told me to drive an empty van for the pickup. I couldn't understand why at first until I saw what was coming our way. They saved the biggest shipment for this time, and it filled the entire van. I was ready for this, what I wasn't ready for was the double-cross of KJ.

149

After the van was loaded and I turned around there KJ stood with a gun pointed right at me. "I'll take those keys off you. It has been fun working with you, but I have a buyer that is going to take all of this off my hands and I'll be sitting on the beach of Tahiti drinking on Hennessy and living life to the fullest."

"Are you out of your mind? Pent will hunt you down. He is not going to let this little betrayal go. Why are you doing this anyway? You've been working with him for so long."

"That's the problem. I've been working with him for so long. Yet he brings in Bret and gives him the area he promised me two years ago. And then there's you, you just began and he's talking about making you his right-hand man already when I'm the one that has been busting my butt to advance for the past three years."
"All you had to do was cut out all the partying and show him you are serious. Don't do this. Just talk to him. I bet he will get where you are coming from."

"Talking is done with. After him telling me that he gave Bret my area and that he will probably have another for me at graduation. I was done talking. Now you don't have to die for someone else's stuff. And I know you would hate for dear Rosalyn there to get hurt. So just hand over the keys. Let me drive off, and by the time you get back to the warehouse, I will be long gone. Which brings me to the next part. I'm going to need your cell phones also. Can't have you calling for help before I can make my escape."

There was no way he was going to be leaving us here or blowing up this deal. I had something on my side that he didn't know about, but he was about to find out really quick. I have the element of surprise on my side and the ability to shift in one second flat.

I proceeded to walk towards him slowly with the keys in my hands. I needed to get as close as possible.

When I was only a few feet away from him he advised me to stop and toss him the keys. Which I did, throwing them with my shifter strength and catching him off guard since he expected a human throw.

By the time he looked down at his chest in shock and back up I was full wolf and on him fast. I bit down on the arm holding the gun, while at the same time using my wolf body to knock him off balance. I was hoping he would go wolf so I could kill him.

"Jordan?" I carefully said from behind him just over the growling in my ears. I could hear Jordan's teeth snapping. He was pacing back and forth in front of Kenneth. He seemed out of control of his body. Did he even want control right now? KJ was slowly crab crawling backward, he threw the keys at Jordan telling him to take them and go.

*He wanted to kill her, he wanted to kill us. Kill everyone and everything we love. Take Rosalyn from us. We should kill him. We need to kill him.*

*-Someone is screaming my name.*

"Jordan! Jordan, don't do this! You have to stop."

*-Rosalyn...do I want to stop?*

*No*

"He's not worth it, if you do this then he still wins, don't lose yourself for him, this is murder and you are not a murderer." I was shocked that her words worked and my wolf gave me back the body. Good thing our clothes shift with us or it would be an awkward conversation we would be avoiding right now.

"Grab the keys, Rosalyn, while 1 tie this piece of horse dung to a tree. The last thing we need is for him to blast my secret to the collective group before we finish this." 1 walked away to do what he asked. "And for you my traitorous roommate I'll be back in the morning to release you."

As we were driving away from the pickup it boggled my mind that he would agree to come back and let KJ loose. "Are you going to come back in the morning and let him loose for real?"

"No, he'll be going to jail tonight. Our room is bugged which he did not know. 1 have so much dirt on him that he couldn't get out of this even if 1 wanted him to. No, he is going down with them also."

"That's good to know. 1 would hate for him to go free after all of this, selling drugs to other students, what lowlife does that. 1 know 1 party all the time, but 1 have never dabbled with drugs and 1 would never encourage someone to do them either, drinking is bad enough. 1 have to be careful who 1 make friends with in the future."

"Or boyfriends for what it's worth."

What could 1 say to that? Nothing. He was right. Trying to make sure 1 don't fall for someone long term 1 end up dating a complete criminal idiot. My taste suck. The best thing for me if 1 can't be with Jordan is to be alone. In the future, 1 may be able to settle down with someone, but for now, my entire judgment is off.

When we arrive back at the warehouse, 1 don't understand why my nerves are all over the place. 1 know 1 have to go inside since I'm the one that has the wire on her. 1 know that I'll be taking down some really bad people. It still doesn't make it less tedious. Before we get out of the car, Jordan grabs my hand. "You ready?"

"As ready as I'll ever be." Taking a deep breath I get out of the car and wait for him to do the same. As we approach the warehouse I make sure to let him know. Not that he didn't already know. That he will be doing all the talking even if they ask me questions, he can take it upon himself to answer for me unless they demand I answer.

When we enter the warehouse it's like a party going on inside. There are so many men here waiting for us.

"Well let me see, three people left to pick up my package but only two return. Can you tell me where is KJ?"

"KJ is a traitor and was about to jack me for the shipment, pulled a gun and everything. Said he had a group of people he had on the line to buy the entire shipment. He had plans to go off and retire in Tahiti."

"I know. At first, I thought that you were a part of it since he is the one that brought you on. Then I thought better of it. He was going to do it the next shipment but I decided this one would be a better trap for him. So I told him that he would be tagging along with you.

Hoping that he succeeded, and I got to have fun tracking him down and killing him slowly for his betrayal. But I guess I was right about you being the perfect right-hand man.

What that fool didn't know was the same person that he made the deal with is the same person I deal with already. So of course when I got that phone call I was surprised they were calling me about KJ and not you. I would've never thought that he would betray me. I guess I know who put the bug in my office." As he walked away he looked back. "I would have put my money on you being on the wrong side of this."

"Well, now you see I'm not. Do you want me to unload?"

153

"Naw, the guys are going to do that. While you were gone Stephan paid me the money. It's over on the table I need you to take it over to the office and put it in the safe in the basement. You get a promotion tonight kid. I'm trusting you with the combo to the safe."

It never got that far, at the moment Jordan turned to go to the table the police and FBI busted in and arrested everyone. Even Jordan and myself. They had to make sure we were not looked at as if we were a part of this takedown. I heard Pent telling Jordan that this had to be KJ's back up plan and not to worry, don't say a word, and wait for the lawyer to show up.

I could have won an Oscar for the performance that I was putting on of being distraught and crying. I played it up. "I don't know why you guys are taking me, I'm just the girlfriend, I don't know anything, I came along to make it to the party on time." Of course, they ignored me. I was even surprised when Pent gave me words of encouragement telling me it's going to be alright and to not worry.

Once we were at the station. They went as far as to put us in a cell, me of course in a separate cell from the guys. They didn't take anyone in to be interrogated except Pent. I could just imagine them telling him about the bugs, the video, and them knowing who is involved. I just pray they don't give him a deal for someone they deem a bigger Fish. It always happens like that in the movies.

It was a long night, but we had to play it smart and be there just as long as everyone else, as to not draw attention to us being released they also released the guys that were there unloading, the guards, and one main man. It was a game they were playing. They would be picking them back up later on.

154

Driving back with Jordan all I could do at the moment was sit there and wonder how to address the elephant or should I say wolf in the car. I looked over at him from the corner of my eye, I noticed when he cut his eye at me, he didn't say anything. I sat there until I couldn't do it anymore, "shifter huh?"

"Yeah. I'm a shifter, from my Mom, my dad's human."

"Hmm, so why didn't you say anything back in freshman year? And why don't you smell like a shifter?" I asked him, turning to face him as best I could while keeping my seat belt on.

"Well to answer your first question I don't tell anyone that I'm a shifter because I want people to like me for me and not for my status. If you like me as a shifter then you should like me as a human. When I get to know a person and I consider them a true friend then I let them know my situation.

Which brings me to your second question. The reason I don't smell like a shifter is that I have a genetic condition where even though I take the traits of a shifter from my Mom. I take the smell of humans from my father.

My parents could never figure out why that happened. I'm an anomaly. When I was little my father developed a spray to help me smell like a wolf. He's a chemist for a large corporation back home. I use it to help my other side feel welcomed, but I don't need to use it for any other reason. I don't mind having my father's genetics."

I looked over and gave him a small smile. "That's kind of cool you know, especially since you want to go into law enforcement. You can do great undercover work for the department. Human or shifter, you are a commodity."

"Yeah, I'm hoping to join the FBI after college and this case just helped steamroll my career on that track. The department has already written me a letter of recommendation for them.

155

And the FBI that was working on the case took my name down for future reference. What about you? Are your plans for the future still the same?"

"Yes, to help other people, just a little more advanced. I don't just want to be a nurse. I want to end up being a charge nurse over pediatrics. I'm in school now to become an RN. After I've done that for two years I can then be promoted to become a charge nurse. It's usually four years but I'm doing two years rotation at the hospital in town which goes towards my credits. I want to go into pediatrics, there are so many babies born sick that need caring for."

"I believe you would be the best nurse in the hospital."

"Thanks for that, but you don't know that much about me."
"I know enough Rosalyn."

What could I say to that? I had my chance and I blew it, to try now to have a relationship is just showing him that I'm just a superficial as the people he tries to stay clear of. All I could do was sit there feeling guilty. I wish I would have gone a different route at the time.

Nothing can change that so I'll just have to move on because there is no way I'm hitting on the guy that I skirted two years ago. When my sister and friends heard about Kenneth, the I told you so's were getting to be a bit much that I actually got me a room in town for a week just so I wouldn't have to be around any of them.

Two weeks have passed since Jordan dropped me off and I have yet to hear from him since. I mean I run into him and he speaks but that's about it. Maybe I should be the one to approach him since I was the one that dumped him without any regard.

Well, not dump since we were only just getting to know each other. Whatever, I might as well get used to more days like this of eating alone in the cafeteria without a special someone beside me. Scooting my food around on my plate. I think I just lost my appetite.

⊕

I heard that everyone who was arrested was being indicted, even the guys that they let go on the premise that they were not going to be in trouble. They even went to the pier and picked up KJ. The good thing was, with all of the evidence from the bugs they didn't need me or Jordan to testify, with how much KJ ran his mouth on his bugs.

"If I sit here will you disappear on me later and avoid me the remainder of the school year?" I look up and see Jordan standing next to the table. I can't help the smile that crosses my face. There has never been anyone I was happier to see. I tried to keep a straight face when I looked up at him.

"I would love for you to sit down it would be the best thing ever. And no. I won't disappear. My Houdini faze is over."
"Could you do me a favor and stand up first."

I didn't know what he wanted me to stand for but at this moment I didn't care. He was here, and I've waited two weeks for this. After I stood it only took a moment for me to find out what he wanted. He took my face between his hands and kissed me right there on the spot. "If and when we do this, then it's us, no more running, I'm playing for keeps. Got it." I was breathless, all I could do was nod my head. That was the kiss that started it all.

Months later after everything was said and done I knew that I could never leave Jordan again. He was the one for me. If only I would have known before it all that he could deal with my brand of crazy we wouldn't have missed two years of being together. I pulled the cell phone he'd gotten me from my pocket and hit the only speed dial number I had saved.

157

"Hey, I was just thinking about you," Jordan answered. And just like that, seven words changed the way my heart felt. There was always going to be some life stress. Fae. Elders. Work. Money problems. But even steadier was Jordan. Over these past weeks, he'd become such an important part of my day. "I like that you were thinking about me." I murmured into the speaker.

"Ohhhh, woman, you're impossible not to think about. Can I take you out tonight after you get off work?"

"Well, I picked up a late shift. Wanna come up to the hospital after your last class?"

"Watch you sashay around in your nurse's outfit? Heck yeah."

"You're such a nerd, that's why I love you." Oh my goodness did I just tell him I love him? What is wrong with me, you do that for the first time in person.

"I love you too, now and forever, and don't you forget it."

"See you later tonight," I said before quickly hanging up.

When Jordan arrived at the hospital I was so happy to see him, I didn't even realize how much I had missed him until I set eyes on him. "You are deeply missed when I'm not near you. I would like to know what you have done to me. How did you get me hooked on you so fast and so hard? What I said on the phone I meant it. I love you Jordan."

"Rosalyn. You mean the world to me. I love you too. Why else would I be sitting here eating this cafeteria food to spend time with you? Ca-fe-te-ri-a food." Jordan said, laughing hard on the last part.

"Watch it buster, our cafeteria serves Grade A mush. You don't get any better than that sir." I said laughing with him. Human or Fae I'm sure lucky.

158

It's getting to the point where I'm feeling guilty about not telling Jordan about my heritage since he has entrusted me with his secrets. I know it's time that I told him what I was and about my family. So tonight is the night I already texted him and told him to meet me at the park.

My friends and I have a special place we like to go to and chill in the summertime when we hang out. I decided to get here early so I could work on what I was going to say to him when he gets here.

"Hey, ladybug. " Jordan says kissing me on my cheek. He sits down with one leg on the inside of the picnic table and the other still on the outside of it facing me, he pulls me closer to him so I'm as snug as I can be in-between his legs. "Not that I don't love spending time with you, but you sounded like what you had to talk to me about was especially important. What's up?"

"We have been dating for a while now, and we kind of dated before. I know that you always ask about my family and I change the subject. Today I don't want to change the subject anymore. I want to tell you about my family. Where they come from, what we are, and why I had to keep it secret this long. But first, let me ask you a question. Do you know all of the different kinds of species that are out here living?"

"Counting them off with his fingers. There are shifters of all kinds, vamps, druids, witches, and warlocks, I think I have them all, except I'm not too certain about the druids."

I sat there for a minute before I responded, "you missed one."

Kissing me on my forehead, "nope ladybug I'm pretty sure I checked off the list."

159

"I can guarantee that you didn't get them all because I'm the one you missed. My family is Fae. My Mom and Aunt Sasha are full-blooded Fae. My siblings and I are half-bloods since our father is human.

There are certain powers that Fae have, we are stronger than humans, more durable, our life span is longer, we have a knack for finding things if we choose to. There are different variations of Fae, my side is supposed to be fire Fae, except only full-blooded Fae can use it. Any questions so far?"

"No, I'm following along, you can keep going."

"Okay. So the Fae have a rule that says we're never supposed to reveal ourselves to anyone that is not in it for the long haul, and even though my Mom married a human and was kicked out of the place she was born, we still live by that rule. So until I knew what we meant to each other I could not tell you without repercussions.

Also, there is a special power the Fae have inside of them when they are born. If you are full-blooded it's guaranteed to manifest at birth and grow and strengthen gradually as you grow up. For half's our power is supposed to manifest when we turn eighteen, however, it doesn't always happen, so before you ask, no I didn't get a power, I'm more human than Fae. At first, it used to bother me, but now it doesn't I have had three years to deal with it."

He sat there for a minute not saying anything, for a moment I thought I had fried his brain with knowledge overload. "Say something, you're freaking me out."

"I'm glad that you shared with me. I have something that I have been wanting to tell you for a minute I just didn't want to freak you out. I don't know if you have any ideas about mates, what they are, and what they mean to a shifter, but you are my mate. Being my mate you are it for me, my life, my heart, my everything.

I know I should have told you earlier since I've known since the first time we kissed Freshman year. Your secret will forever be safe with me. I would nor could I ever do anything to bring you hurt or harm intentionally."

"So what you are saying is this is a forever kind of love," giving him a kiss on the cheek, "I can work with that."

"That's good to hear you say. I don't know what I would do without you in my corner."

"Ditto. How about we get out of here and go by the diner and grab something to eat?"

He gave me a long lingering kiss before answering, "I can eat."

"Will, I ever get to see you shift?" He looked at me and I knew what he was about to say. "I mean without all the drama behind it. Just you, me, and him."

"Whenever you want, just say the word."

I had to think on this, I wanted it to be special. Also, I didn't know if I would need to have Rosie there like she had me for when Augustas shifted for the first time so that his Bear would know the difference between the two of us. Come to think of it, "Hey, I was wondering since I'm an identical twin would your wolf need to see Rosie too, so he won't get mixed up between the both of us?"

"No, it should be fine. Trust and believe he has your scent planted in his head. There will be no mistaking it for anyone else. Why do you ask?"

"Only because when Augustas shifted for Rosie the first time I needed to be there so he wouldn't get confused, he couldn't understand that there were two of us and not the same person twice, if that makes sense, Augustas wanted him to see us both together."

"I mean I don't think it would be a problem with regard to your scent, but Augustas had a great idea, it may be good for him to see that it's two of you so he won't get confused from afar if he happens to see Rosie with Augustas and be ready to go on the attack. He would think twice and investigate. So let's do that, set it up, and let me know."

I smiled up at him, "I'll do that."

When I got back to the room I was happy to find my sister there. I told her about the situation with Jordan, when I told her he was a wolf shifter you could have knocked her over with a feather. Of course, she was happy for me. I even told her that I told him about the family, but didn't reveal any powers that she had, just that I didn't have any.

She was happy to hear that I had found someone to be in my life, she even made the comment about maybe he can keep me out of parties. We'll see, I'm who I am.

Jordan picked me up later that night to take me out to dinner. It was on my mind heavy to tell him what is going on with the Fae leaders not liking me and my sister and why. He took me to a genuinely nice rib place. Their ribs were delicious.

What is better than telling the man of your dreams that someone is trying to take that dream away. No matter how many times I tried to let it out I couldn't tell him and spoil the mood.

Later that night after he had dropped me off. While I laid in bed, I had one thing on my mind. I'm the luckiest woman in the world. This has been the busiest first half of my junior year.

I'm so awaiting spring break so I can get the needed rest that I so much deserve.

I had wanted to go skiing but due to the situation of the threat that is lingering over our heads. Rosie vetoed that real quick and said it was best if we went home instead.

⟨⊕⟩

Jordan decided that we should go to the beach today and lay out and relax, give us a break from school and studying. I was laying on my stomach enjoying the breeze and him rubbing up and down my back. When he gave me the best surprise ever.

"I was thinking that since you're serious about not going skiing. That I could just go home with you and kick it with your family and get to know them better."

"That would be great. Have I told you lately that you are the best boyfriend ever?"

"Every day babe, every day."

While on spring break Jordan made sure to get me up at four a.m. every morning to go for a run. To improve on my stamina he said. Even though I agreed with him spending spring break to improve on my stamina was not what I had in mind. At first. I didn't enjoy it, but after a while, I could see how much I needed it. I won't admit that to him, I don't need his head getting big on me.

Jordan thought it would be fun if I took him on a tour around the farm and town. I didn't know what was going on in his head. But he kept asking questions about the people and how are they with shifters. While we were on a picnic the next day my questions were answered.

163

Laying back with his head in my lap, he looked up at me as if he had a question on his mind. "I know we've never thought about the future. We still have a year and a half left. I just wanted to know where do you see us living after graduation?"

"I never thought about it. All my life I thought I would get my degree, move back home, and work at the local hospital." I looked at him and rubbed his head. "Now I have you in my life, taking that into consideration is important to me. What the future holds has been on my mind also."

"Why didn't you ever say anything?"

"I didn't want to push. Like you said we still have time left before we have to make a decision."

"Honestly, I don't. I'm going into law enforcement, so I need to find a place to do my ride alongs and you usually do that with the station you're going to be working at. I need to do this during summer vacation. With that being said, we need to discuss where we're going to end up."

"We're going to end up wherever you want to start your career."

"Sweetie."

I held up my hand to stop what he was going to say. "Look I can be a nurse in any hospital in the world. Your career is in law enforcement, there are certain things you have to worry about. Do they have an occupancy, would you fit in with the staff, will it be the best precinct to help you advance to the Federal level. I love you J, so wherever you go I go, and that's final."

He smiled up at me and shook his head, "I guess it's good then that I applied for my rotation with the Vermont police department and was told that I can do my ride along the summer of my senior year."

164

I could have burst a bubble I was so happy, not having to leave my family. "Are you being serious right now? What about you moving far away from your family? Maybe we should find a place in the middle of both families and relocate there."

"First, yes I'm profoundly serious the paperwork is already done, and as far as my family they are happy for me, wolf shifters are not like others we are solitary creatures that seek to establish our pack, you being my mate is the beginning of that. You are my family now. If you wanted to move to a halfway point then we can do that, but not for the reason of being close to my family."

"I'm the luckiest woman in the world. You are a great man Jordan."

"I try to be. Come on, let's get cleaned up so we can make it back in time to see if that Sow has her baby."

"You're taking on this whole farming thing. My real-life cowboy."

He couldn't help but laugh, swinging me around at the same time, "you bet your pretty little butt I am."

CD

This Spring break was the best one I have ever had. I came back to school more relaxed and at ease than I had ever felt. Months had gone past since the raid, the last thing on my mind was KJ, so when I got a subpoena to testify against him it was not a welcoming sight.

They had me down as his long-term girlfriend. Well, ex-girlfriend. What I witnessed wasn't much. I never saw him dealing drugs. Why I had to be involved I didn't know. Didn't they have enough with the recordings?

When I appeared in court they asked me about the food truck that was at the Rave. And if I observed drugs being sold. Which I didn't.

They even asked me if I ever met a girl named Valarie who fought in an underground fight club that was being investigated for illegal dealings. When I informed them that I had met her and she approached me at the club one night I was out with Kenneth.

They told me her body was found in a dumpster in Delaware. They asked me if I knew how that happened, answering honestly I told them no I didn't. I do know that I gave her number to Kenneth, which I didn't mention, I would hate for them to think that I set her up or something of that nature.

I wondered if he had anything to do with her death. I was also questioned on rather or not I observed Kenneth selling drugs. Which the answer was no. I knew he sold weed but that is legal so I didn't see anything wrong with it. When I was done at court that day. I promised myself that I would never put myself in a situation like that ever again.

After the entire KJ fiasco, I was awaiting something else to happen. I was totally grateful when the remainder of junior year went off without any hitches getting in the way. I was still glowing with happiness and enjoying Jordan.

When this school year ended I was glad to be going home and taking a breather from all of the stresses of the world and school. Junior year was not what I expected it to be. I need this time off from everything.

Summer vacation is going to be me regrouping and finding myself again to get back to the old me. I have lost Ros somewhere along the way and I no longer see myself when I look in the mirror, I see a stranger and that's not good. I'm going to use this time to steal me back from the edge of destruction.

∞

I've been at home for about a week now, I'm enjoying myself immensely being around the family, laughing and hanging out. Just remembering where I came from.

Right now I'm in the kitchen listening to my Mom and her sister banter over who can cook the best.

"Rosalyn, you have to be the judge here. You've had your mom's dried out fried Chicken. Then there is my juicy mouthwatering smack your lips fried Chicken. So tell me who is the best cook of the Fried Chicken?" I looked back and forth between the both of them, my Mom giving me the where does your allegiance lay look and my aunt Sasha looking with a smirk on her face. "I know honey. Go on burst her little bubble." Said Aunt Sasha.

"Cook-off." Is how I answered.

My Mom looked at me, tilting her head like a puppy would do when you say something to them they don't seem to understand. "What did you say?"

"I said you two should have a cook-off. Both of you fry up some Chicken. Put it out without telling anyone who's Chicken is whose and watch and see what everyone says. They will be honest because they won't know that they are being judges. You will get an honest response to both your Chicken."

Aunt Sasha jumped from her chair. "That sounds like a great idea. Sunday dinner will be the night since everyone comes over anyway, I'll cook one platter of Chicken and you can cook the other. We will use the same type of platter for both, that way no one can get hints as too who's Chicken is who's. We will put our name on the bottom with a label. Rosalyn, since you know the plan so you won't be judging you'll carry the platters in for us."

My Mom turned to my auntie and stuck out her hand, "deal." My aunt grabbed it and shook, "deal." This was going to be so much fun watching their faces while people eat. Making sure everyone gets a piece off each platter will be the challenge. I started to bring it up. However looking at them, I thought better of it, nope not going down that road. It seemed though I didn't need to.

167

My Mom spoke up, "to make sure that everyone gets a piece of both we will make even number pieces of chicken. That way when the first platter is empty they have no choice but to take their seconds from the other platter. We will listen to see who's the best by the things they say during dinner."

As my Mom was talking my aunt was bobbing her head in agreement. The idea will work since there has never been a Sunday dinner where everyone doesn't eat two or three pieces of Chicken, the only argument will be they will have to settle for only two until the other platter is empty. Of course, I know how they are about their food so I will have a separate platter in the oven on standby.

"You both have to Fae swear not to tell anyone what is going on," they both looked at me as if I had wounded them, and I looked at them with that don't give me that look.

"Fine." They said in unison." I swear on my power as full-blooded born Fae that if I break the trust of my competitor. She may seek revenge and I will not retaliate against her."

"Really Abigail," my Aunt Sasha looked at my Mom, "Why you would tell her about that oath anyway."

"She was eight, how was I supposed to know that one day she would use it against us."

I just smiled at them and walked away. Yes, this was going to be so much fun, no cheating for them. Sunday dinner was absolutely amazing and funny. I couldn't help chuckling every time someone ate a piece of Chicken and said how good it was. When the second platter was served everyone did the same thing, gave praise no more or less than the first tray.

I could see my Mother and aunt's face fallen when they realized it will not be a clear winner. That they would tie. What they didn't know was. If they were thinking right they would have made me swear not to tell.

I told everyone in the family about the bet and we came to the same conclusion. If we want their good cooking from now on, then no one loses. When dinner was over and we were in the kitchen cleaning up, I overheard them talking about the end result of their contest.

My aunt and mom decided that it was best not to worry about who's better and just enjoy the outcome of having their food eaten. I just rolled my eyes. I give it maybe a month and they will be comparing something else and arguing about who is better.

# CHAPTER 17

After dinner, while we were sitting around talking as perusal our after Sunday dinner routine. My dad decided to bring up the elephant in my life. "Rosalyn? I've been wondering rather or not you've been feeling any different inside? Do you feel as if your inner power is getting stronger?"

"No, dad. Like I told you all last year. I think I'm more human than Fae, maybe in the womb, Rosie was given all the Fae DNA and I was given none. Maybe that's why she has that weird power, from taking all of it herself, and not sharing."

"Tell us honestly how do you feel about that?" Asked my mother.

"At first I was upset. I mean terribly upset, then it turned into denial of the fact that I would never have anything special like everyone else. After Sophomore year it turned from frustration to annoyance that at every turn someone kept asking me how I felt or if I thought my power will manifest soon." She started to say something, but I waved her off. "I'm over it now mom. So you asking me is not bothersome to me. I can tell you how if you want."

My aunt answered before either of my parents could. "Truly you are old enough to handle your own business. If you don't want to share your parents will understand." She looked at them with a look that would shut anyone down. My father's sister Aunt Samantha has never been one to tangle with. "Won't you?" She directly asked the question to my parents.

"Of course." My father said automatically. However, my mother being the most stubborn person I have ever laid eyes on was not having it. I saw the look she gave so I decided to guide this conversation away from an argument. "I don't mind Auntie.

Thank you. As I was saying, by the end of my Sophomore year I was lost, yeah that's a good word to use. I was partying all the time trying to forget the fact that I'm a Fae failure."

My father interrupted me, "sweetheart you're not a Fae failure."

"Dad, that's how you feel. I'm telling you how I felt. Now don't get me wrong, I don't have a problem being human. How could I when I have the best example of a human as a father. I had a problem with the let-down of my power not manifesting. I was raised knowing that I was supposed to inherit this magical power. I was sold on it, waited on it for eighteen years.

When it didn't happen it was a devastating blow to my sense of who I am. I was supposed to have the DNA makeup of two different species, however, I don't. It was a letdown a disappointment I couldn't seem to wrap my mind around. Why me?"

I stood to grab me a drink of juice off the bar before continuing my tale and finally letting my family in. "Would anyone like a drink before I continue?" They all said no, I think they were just anticipating my story and was too anxious to drink. "Like I was saying, my self-worth was less than zero by the middle of Sophomore year. Before the lecture begins, let me first say that I know already, and none of you can be more disappointed in me than I'm in myself.

I turned to partying, hanging out, and drinking, nothing heavy just beer but I did drink it, and I have been partying every weekend for months. Rosie and Danielle have tried talking to me. They tried to turn me back around. But the only thing I could think was how could Rosie understand. She's walking around with a power she doesn't even want or appreciate.

That in itself brought me down even more. I figured since I was keeping up with my grades then it was no reason to bother anyone, if I was worse off there would be no way I would still be maintaining good grades, working in the hospital, or functioning on a daily basis.

I didn't stop doing what I was doing, and it has been going on even this year. But something happened. Lately, there have been a bunch of overdoses at school and even though I don't take drugs of any kind it still made me look at myself.

Since I attended the same parties that those kids did. Even though I wasn't responsible for them using drugs I just didn't like the person that was looking back out the mirror at me.

The kind of person that would ignore what is going on around her just so she can have fun and not even really fun, but artificial. I stopped hanging with the crew and drew into myself, so I didn't have to feel anything. I even dumped a nice guy freshman year, so I didn't have to try to pretend to be happy when I wasn't."

I made excuses about not wanting to hang because they are all coupled up, they would tell me to invite my male friend. But I made him safe, we weren't like that at first. We chill together, have fun, but it was not meant to be serious.

So I would tell them he didn't want to go even though I didn't even invite him, and it was easy because he didn't know them. The type of friendship we had made it convenient hanging with him, it was easy.

Anyway, I'm drifting. That relationship is long over and I have Jordan back in my life, which helped me to I took a long look at Rosalyn and the person I used to be and the person I am now. I know I need a change so that is why I came home instead of staying at school.

I need to get myself together. I need to be surrounded by family. I need to remember what is more important than having problems. Well in my case not having them."

By the time I finished my Mom and aunts had tears running down their cheeks, they got up and hugged me tight, they hugged me so long that I just let the tears flow. It felt just as I did when I was a little girl and needed to be shown some special kind of love from the women in this family.

I don't know how long we stayed there, but it felt great. After everyone moved back, my dad slid in beside me and hugged me also.

"My dear little bug, why didn't you come and talk to us? We would have understood."

"I know dad, it's just until now there was no way to put my feelings into words. My emotions were all over the place. Until now I wouldn't have been able to articulate very well what I wanted to say. Better late than never."

He squeezed my hands, "better late than never."

After my story to my family, I felt as if a heavyweight was lifted from me and I could see clearer. I know what I have to do when I get back to school. Focus. I knew my next move, tomorrow I'll be calling the clinic and seeing if I can get in a few shifts to work while I'm here. That will keep me somewhat busy.

The rest of the time I'll use it to work with my family on the farm. Go to the beach in town or to the city pool, just enjoy my summer, let the other stuff work itself out. I can say that I'm one lucky girl to have a family like the one I have.

I awoke the next morning fresh and renewed and ready to start the day. When I arrived downstairs my mother was in the kitchen cooking.

Pancakes, bacon, sausage, hash browns, grits, and homemade biscuits. Recovery breakfast. I couldn't help but smile. Growing up whenever one of us had a bad day, or something happened to us that would cause us some kind of heartache.

The next morning when we would come down for breakfast there would be my Mom cooking a recovery breakfast to add to the healing process. I just walked up to her and kissed her on the cheek. I knew she would know what I was saying. And of course, since she was famous for these breakfasts most of the family had shown up to eat.

My dad walked into the kitchen kissed me on my forehead, "how are you feeling this morning daughter?"

"I'm fine dad, thanks for the ask. Now all I need is some of mom's cooking and I'll be right as rain." I looked at my cousins Mark and Markese, they are the twin sons of Seth, who is a bear shifter and Auntie Sasha.

They also have a little sister name Randa, she is my age, and goes to Parks University also. She just doesn't socialize. She's a book worm. Focused on returning home after graduation to help out. "So twinzies what are you two doing the rest of the day?"

Mark stopped eating long enough to look at me, but he didn't stop chewing. Markese was the one to answer. "We're going out to the field to see how the crops are doing, then we will be heading in town to pick up some seeds for a new crop we're going to be planting in the east field."

"Mind if I tag along? My shift at the clinic doesn't start until six tonight." They both hunched their shoulders as to say they didn't care. Why answer when you're too busy trying to eat your weight in food.

CD

I always enjoy spending time at the clinic in the maternity ward, looking at the babies brings me joy to my heart. Even though I didn't get my healing powers I decided I was not going to let that deter me from my dream of working with babies.

They are innocent, loving, and have the new baby smell. I would love to work in the intensive care ward but without being able to help the babies it would just break my heart. While I was eating my lunch nurse Evans came and asked me if I would work in the E.R. after my break. I told her I would. If they were pulling me from the maternity floor, they were getting their butts kicked down there.

While I was in the E.R. I felt as if someone was watching me, the little hairs on the back of my neck kept tingling. But whenever I looked around everyone was busy doing something, and I couldn't see anyone.

No one was paying attention to me. It went on all night to the point that instead of walking home like I usually do in the summer to unwind. I called my father and asked him to pick me up. When I got in the car my skin was still crawling from the feeling of being watched.

"Honey, you don't look so good. What happened?" Asked my Dad.

"Nothing really, I just had a feeling of being watched all day, but I saw no one when I looked around, it felt creepy, so I didn't feel comfortable walking home."

"You decided right. Next time you should call your mom or aunt to come up and check it out, they may be able to sense something you can't." Thanks, dad your right.

I couldn't help but look out the side mirror as we drove away, I could have sworn there was a person standing on the sidewalk, I couldn't tell if it was man or woman or if they were looking this way. Something deep inside though told me I was looking at the person that had been watching me all night.

The same thing happened again for the next three nights. That strange feeling of being watched. So it wasn't just in the E.R. it was anywhere I was in the hospital. I thought about the picture of the letter that was still on my phone. I was wondering if I should just call my Mom up here, but I didn't want her to come up because I had the jitters.

However, I was so stressed out I did call my Aunt Sasha though. She said for me not to call my dad for a ride, to leave the hospital as if I was walking home and she'll be waiting outside for me. The hope was that whoever it is would follow me outside. If it's anyone at all, I could be just losing my mind.

I was a bundle of nerves for the rest of my shift. I couldn't get my mind off what may or may not happen when I walk out the door tonight. To make things worse I was focused on my job and Aunt Sasha possibly being outside I didn't even pay attention to the fact of if I was feeling watched. After my shift, while I was walking through to grab my coat I tried to see if I had that creepy feeling, there was nothing. Go figure.

When I got outside I tried not to look for my aunt and make it obvious that someone was waiting for me. I started down the street. Hoping the person showed themselves. However, when I made it to the corner of the building, my Aunt Sasha was there for me.

"Hey, Auntie."

"Hey, there love. Did you feel anything?"

"To be honest I was so anxious that I didn't even pay attention. But as you can see no one jumped out at me so I guess I have been imagining things this entire time. I'm sorry for dragging you out on a blank trip for my overactive imagination."

She stopped and looked at me, "don't you ever be sorry for caring for yourself. Let me tell you something. Even though your extra power never manifested. That doesn't mean you don't have any Fae powers you do. You were born with them, so if you thought you felt something, you did. You must always pay attention to that. Our Fae intuition is on point."

"Thanks, Auntie. I just hate that you have to walk all the way home with me." She looked at me and shook her head, "and here I thought you knew me better than that, I might not drive but there is no way I'm going to be walking home. Your cousin Mark is parked down the street. Come on let's catch our getaway ride."

When I got to the car I noticed that it was not only Mark in the car, it was also Jefferson and Darcie. My aunt came prepared for whatever was going to go down. That's why growing up I always called her a silent attacker. We never knew when It would happen but whenever my mom or someone else really upset her.

Us kids would just sit back and watch and wait. We never would see her do it but orange hair dye in my Mom's shampoo one time. I bet that was her. Now if I would have called my Mom she would have come in the hospital guns a blazing asking who looking for her daughter. My mother does not play behind the scenes when it comes to her kids.

As I slid in the car next to Jefferson. Smiling at them, "I know I don't have to say it, but thanks guys for showing up for me."

Jefferson squeezed my hand, "anytime, anyplace."

"What he said," replied Darcie.

177

The next two days went by without a hitch. No feelings of being watched nothing at all. This was my last night at the clinic I'll be returning to school in two days and wanted to make sure I spent those days with my family. Halfway through my shift, a woman approached me. When I looked at her I felt as if she was not human for some reason. It was a quick strange feeling.

She stopped in front of me, "You don't know me, Rosalyn, I'm your mother's sister Melusine and I couldn't go to your house without being discovered by my family. So I came here to warn you your home is going to be attacked tonight. You don't have to believe me however I wish you would."

"What are you talking about?" I asked trying to see any form of deception.

"Listen, you need to warn your parents. I'm from Azurion and there was a buzz going around about attacking your family to get to you girls. I wanted to come and warn you early, but I couldn't get away. You need to go."

I looked at her and took off running, I tried calling my Mom through our family mind link, but I didn't get an answer. Running out the door I tried all of them one by one with no success. I then pulled my cell out of my pocket and called the house.

No one picked up the phone. I wished I would have had a car. It will take me at least twenty minutes to run home. I had to do what I had to do so I took off, constantly dialing the number as I went begging in my head for someone to pick up.

When I got to the house the scene in front of me had to be out of an action movie. Things like this don't happen in real life. Icicles were flying, fireballs flying, shifters dodging and attacking people dressed in combat gear with a face mask on. But they had to be Fae only they can shoot things like this from their hands.

178

I needed to help but what would I do? I have my Jiu-jitsu skills. I hope that's good enough to help. I went running towards the house and when I came into view I locked eyes with my Mom. I started to run towards her when my world went blank, I was grabbed around my waist, lifted in the air, and thrown over someone's shoulder.

# CHAPTER 18

Someone had put a sack over my head and pinned my arms to my body. I can't get away so I screamed as loud as I could. I knew it didn't matter when I felt rope going around my body, my hands were tied behind my back, and I was thrown into the trunk of a car.

I knew it was the trunk from one of the guys telling someone to put me in it. When the car started and they proceeded to drive I knew I was in trouble.

*Mom are you there?*

*Yes, sweetie, I'm here. Quickly I need you to count and pay attention to the turns and call them out.*

That is what I did, I started counting whenever we turned I called out left or right. I don't know how long we drove, but it felt like a long time with my head covered.

*Mom, we've stopped.*

*What's happening?*

*I don't know we're just stopped. My head is covered and my hands are tied behind my back.*

*Try to get loose. You can do it, just focus on the knot. Try twisting your hands back and forth to see if you can loosen the hold.*

*Okay. I'll try.*

"Did you do it yet?"

180

*Mom, there are two of them their talking. One is asking the other if he did something yet. I don't know what.*

*Okay sweetie, what else?*

"No, I had to get out of there fast. I'm about to do it now."

*He's coming.*

When the trunk opened I started to say something, but before I could I felt a prick. *He stuck me, mom.* I don't know what happened after that. I just remembered trying to talk to my Mom then nothing.

When I came to I didn't know where I was at, but I knew that I have to be still until I hear something. I don't know how long I've been here either. *Mom, mom are you there? Mom, please answer. Aunt Sasha, Dad. Please someone answer.*

Wherever I am my link doesn't work? Or is it what they stuck me with? Don't panic Rosalyn, calm down. Your family will find you, one way or another. Markese and Jefferson are the best trackers in the family. I know I can be found from the last position I was at. Or what if they drove more after he put me out. What am I going to do?

All of a sudden the cover was pulled off my head, bright lights were blasting me in the face, which made me close my eyes instantly from being in the dark so long. Turning my head I opened my eyes slowly to let them adjust to my surroundings. One thing I noticed was the walls were shining.

After a few more minutes and being able to fully focus I saw why. Steel plates were on the walls surrounding me. That is why I can't reach out to my family. I'm tied up and stuck.

"We need you to do us a favor and once you do it we will let you go."

I looked around, trying to see somebody, anybody. "Who are you?"

"Who we are is not important. You doing what we want and leaving out of here in one piece is more important."

"What do you want from me?"

"We need you to use your power."

"What are you talking about? I don't have any powers."

"I find that hard to believe, your twin came into her powers early, you two share the same DNA so we know that if she got it you are a liar and you have it also. We aren't here to harm you, sorry about the way we had to take you, but we need to get this done. Aren't you tired as a Fae of having to hide? Of being thought less of because you share the blood of a human? It can all stop tonight if you just use your power and help us to bring down the veil that is blocking the humans from seeing Azurion."

"That is all fine and good, it still doesn't neglect the fact that I do not have power, I'm not like my sister."

"That's impossible. The prophecy states that twin girls will be born with the power of Telekinesis that will destroy the veil and reveal the Fae to the world. We need that to happen and we need it to happen sooner than later. It's better to work with us and not against us Rosalyn."

"With you or against you. I don't have powers plain and simple. Even if I wanted to take down this veil and increase your chances of fulfilling this so-called prophecy and being able to come out to the world. I'm not your girl."

"I have to make a call, and for the record, I don't believe you, my intel is correct. I think you are just working with your mother's family to disrupt our plans, falling in line. Well, it won't work.

When I get back if you want to walk out of here you will stop playing around and do what I ask you to do."

The mystery person started to walk away, "wait, if you brought me here to take down the veil does that mean I'm in Azurion?"

"Not that it matters, you are not in Azurion. You are of course close enough to do what we want. I'll give you a few hours to think about it. When I get back it will be now or never. And trust me I have nothing to lose. You don't want me to show you what will happen if I don't get what I want." And with that, he was gone.

I sat there thinking not about his request but about how I could get free, by the feel of the cords that have me tied to the chair tells me they're shifter enforced. I have nothing. If only I had my powers, but even with those what could, I do. It's not like I'm full Fae and can shoot fire from my hands.

I'm sitting here wondering how this happened. Well I know how it happened I just can't believe I may never be able to see my family ever again. I'm not old enough to die. I haven't even lived yet. You have to be the dumbest person in the world if you don't believe a person you are threatening with death for them to do something for you.

Mother of earth, air, water, and fire bless me on this day to hold my head up high and deal with this as a one true Fae. A little Fae prayer never hurts anyone. I opened my eyes and looked around trying to see if I could see something. I tried to tune in and see if I could hear anything. I tried scooting the chair, unfortunately, it's made of metal and with the progress, I was making I'll be to the lights by this time next year.

At least if I make it to the lights I might be able to knock them down so I can see all of the areas I'm in. While doing my next set of scoots there was a loud crash. I would have been happy thinking it was me sadly I was nowhere near the lamps.

Which meant he was back, and this was the end for me unless I can fake him out.

"I don't know about you, but I was thinking that you would like to go home now?"

"Jefferson? Please tell me that the voice I recognized is Jefferson and not another criminal with the same voice as my cousin. Okay, I'm babbling because I'm nervous that I'm about to die for not having a requested power."

After I closed my mouth long enough to let the person answer, I realized that it was my cousin, since he was untying me at this moment. I wanted to cry so badly, but there was no way. I always hated the girls in the movies that would break down crying instead of getting away from the criminals.

Not me, I'll cry later when I'm at home. As soon as I was untied I jumped up and ran past the lights I didn't know where I was going but something told me that was the way out. Jefferson was right beside me. If it looked like I was making a wrong turn he would tug on my arm to guide me the correct way.

When we finally arrived outside. I took a look around and found that I had been in a cave. Where I had no idea, I have never been to this area before. My Mom and dad were outside waiting for me when we got out there.

"You all head to the car I need to leave these people a little gift." Said, my Mom. I started to say something but changed my mind. My dad hugged me around my shoulder and guided me towards the car.

When my Mom arrived at the car, she was huffing mad. "I think it's best if we were to get out of here and quickly." When I went to ask her why as we were pulling away I got my answer when a big blast went off. I turned around to look out the back window.

I saw a huge fireball shooting up in the sky. "Mom, did you just blow up that cave?"

"You darn right I did. No one messes with my children. That should leave them a message. Rosalyn, did you see who it was?"

"Nope, he had lights shining in my face the entire time so I wouldn't see his face. He did, however, say something very strange, he wanted me to stop lying and use my powers to take down the veil. When I told him that he was mistaken and I had no powers he told me that I was a liar, and then he proceeded to proclaim some prophecy that involves me and Rosie, and with that alone, he knows I have powers and I'm just lying. He gave me an hour to reconsider and if I didn't he insinuated that would be my last hour."

If I thought my mother was upset. My father was white knuckle holding the steering wheel, with his jaw tight and eyes squinting. "Dad, if you don't calm down you are going to bust a vein."

He took a deep breath. "I know baby girl. It just ticks my buttons someone threatening my daughter and me not there to shut him up."

"I know dad. One good thing about this is you all found me. By the way, not that I'm not extremely grateful. How did you find me?"

My Mom shook her head. "It was part tracking and part luck. We followed your directions with the counts and directions. When we got to the spot where you were put out, we were lost on which way to go from there. Jefferson is good but not that good without any traces.

When they put you out they eliminated your aura which we would have been able to track. Markese was able to catch a light scent of a musk smell, that brought us deep into the woods.

He lost it though about ten minutes later. As you know Full-blooded Fae have a certain aura about them usually. Unless you are a certain distance from them you wouldn't even notice they're around, when two full-blooded Fae is in the range of each other they can feel each other. Which was not handy at all in this instance.

Jefferson's power of reading auras came in handy. The guy that took you Jefferson was able to see his aura. It led us in the direction of which way he went on foot. Just not to you. By the time we made it to your destination, the aura was thinning out. We were close but didn't exactly know where.

This is where the luck came in at, we were standing in the middle of the woods lost when we saw some car lights leaving out the woods. So we just walked in that direction. It took us a while but in the end, we found that cave you were in and the rest is history."

I laid my head on my Mom's shoulder. We were sitting in the backseat with Markese. My dad was driving while Jefferson was riding in the passenger seat. Not to spark my dad off again I whispered to my Mom. "I was scared I was going to die tonight."

"I could only imagine sweetheart. I was worried also. You better believe I was ready to burn the whole world down to find you. I don't like this. Someone taking you like that or attacking the house to get to you or Rosie."

At that, I sat up, "Rosie. How did I forget about Rosie? Have anyone went after her?"

My Mom giggled. "If they do, I believe it will be the last thing they do on earth. Augustas is not one to be reckoned with, he has been following her around so much, she called to see if she could get Theresa to put a sleeping spell on him.

186

We called Rosie as soon as you were taken to warn her, she wanted to come home and help look for you, but I assured her by the time she made the drive we would already have you back. Give her a call, I know she is probably waiting on pins and needles."

After the phone call to my sister's Rosie and Sapphire letting them know I was rescued and safe, the next thing I know my Mom was shaking me woke. "We're here."

I sat up looking around. I know I was involved in something that was taxing on the head, but not enough to be confused as to what my house looks like. "We're where?"

My dad turned around in the front seat, "since the house was attacked and they are looking for you girls, we thought it best if we moved a little bit closer to the school, just in case. So we rented this cabin that's off the beaten path near the town and school, but far enough that you girls still have your privacy. Also, we're having a fence put up around the farm so that what happened will be less likely to happen again."

Getting out the car my Mom expanded on that, "the fence will not encase the woods, if they go through there to get to the house they will have a different surprise at the border of our land. We also have cameras put in with alarms so that if someone passes a certain spot we will be notified. We came too close this time to being eliminated, and one of our own being taken from us." With that, my Mom and Dad gave me another huge hug along with Jefferson and Markese.

"Markese."

"It doesn't even have to be said. If it wasn't for Jay coming home when he did we would have never known that they were out there. And if they weren't so dumb as to not know that it was not a delivery person coming to the house, but a family member, we still wouldn't have known, ain't no telling what they would have done or tried to do to Jay so he wouldn't warn us."

"And he said delivering for that bakery wouldn't amount to anything," I replied. "I must say, this has been the longest summer vacation I have ever experienced. I'm kind of glad to be back at school, at least I have all my friends and my sisters."

"Speaking of, they should be here in the next fifteen minutes to pick you up." Replied my dad. "We thought it best if they came here, instead of us driving you to the school. I mean what Senior wants to be driven back to school by her parents?"

When everyone arrived, I wasn't shocked that the entire crew showed up to get me. We are a team, and with that, they are going to take this protection detail that my Mom is currently putting them on very seriously. I can do this for six months. Having them follow me around then I'll be away from here and doing my own thing.
I wasn't shocked to see Jordan there either. If I knew my sister she called and told him what was going on. He walked up and gathered me in his arms, it felt like a warm blanket being wrapped around me. He looked down at me.

"What happened love?"

"Remember when I told you about the secrecy of the Fae and how they hold that sacred above all things?"

"Yeah, that's still crazy to me, I doubt anyone would care that there are Fae in the world."

"That part...The thing I found out tonight is, because of some stupid prophecy they have decided that my sister and I are detrimental to their livelihood if we don't help them to achieve their end game.

He stood straight up and looked at me in shock, "what are you talking about Rosalyn?"

"Apparently there is a prophecy that says. A set of twins will be born that will bring destruction to the Fae and apparently that is my sister and I. The guys that took me tonight want that destruction to happen."

"Well, that just means we have another adventure to face together. I'm not a runner and I'm here for the long haul, so if the Fae want a fight then they will get a fight. This is the last time someone will get close enough to put their hands on you."

# CHAPTER 19

Senior year is upon me and outside of wondering when and if some crazy Fae is going to come out of the woodworks and attack, I'm glad to be back at school. I mean I love visiting the family but sometimes they can be too much.

It's my last year of school and I have a feeling it's going to be a great one. Ever since the attack, the family has been on pins and needles about me and my sister.

My name is Rosalyn Dodson and I'm a healer. My Fae power finally manifested after the summer break. It was not as cool as my twin sisters Rosie's. But it's what I have always wanted. I can heal with a touch, so my nursing degree will come in handy when I finally graduate. This would have been the best year ever if not for someone wanting to force me to do something for them.

With everything that happened, I guess the stress of it brought out my powers. I discovered that not only can I heal ANYTHING. Got a sick plant, flower, garden, whatever, come get me I got you. Have a sick relative, friend, or even foe, again come get me I got you.

Not that I can actually tell anyone and use it outside of my family. Yet still, the thought is good enough for me. At least I get to do more at the hospital.

Oh yeah. I can also dream walk. What I thought was a dream about Jordan last year was a weird form of dream walking. What I think is a dream is actually what is going to happen in the near future. The problem is I don't know-how. I'll have to keep watch, look at similar signals, remind myself that if it's DeJa'Vu then most likely I need to pay attention. I dream of the future.

I live it whenever I fall asleep and dream. My dreams are no longer my own. It doesn't happen every night thank goodness. I also don't know what triggers them. It's not like I have so much going on that I can't deal with another power. I guess it's true what they say be careful of what you wish for.

How did I figure out I can dream walk? Because I'm living the dream I had two nights ago. Me telling my parents about my power of healing, the excitement they were going to show. It then showed how overbearing they were going to be, saying they might need to increase the security around me to pertain to outside people that are not my friends since they have classes. Just to make sure that if the other power manifest itself also no one comes for me.

And here it is. My dream. My parents were so excited for me that they became overbearing. I remember when I was a little jealous of the attention that Rosie was getting due to her having her power until that attention has now been turned on me. I did wish that Rosie had come with me to tell them.

She would have taken some of the focus off me. One thing though, my mother was able to help me realize that the healing properties that I possess are not limited to only humans. I convinced them not to bring on anyone else since it was only one power. Glad I didn't tell them about the dream thing. I might have a full guard right now.

I was also happy that my parents will be leaving to head home today. Even though the cabin they rented was a nice size, sharing it with your parents is not a fun situation. No privacy at all. My father constantly coming to the window or door when I and Jordan were sitting outside trying to enjoy each other's company. My Mom asking too many embarrassing questions to Jordan. You would have thought she worked for the C.I.A.

With the grilling, she was giving him. She didn't do that when he came home last Spring break. Maybe she didn't think it was going to last then. When she got to his family I had to intervene. Letting her know that he is an only child and his parents are still living and are currently residing in Denmark. Letting her know that was the end of that.

⊕

Classes are going great I'm so excited about the nursing rotation that I have signed up for, now I can do more to help patients, a little push here and there can never harm. It's the wintertime practically and if anyone knows anything about me it's the fact that I don't do well in the wintertime. I like to sit under a blanket and drink as much tea as I can get my hands on.

I was sitting around the common area minding my own business when Rosie decided that we would go out into the woods behind the football field so she could do some practicing on her skills. Not that I didn't love my sister, but I would rather be hanging with Jordan, he has become my calm within the storm that is my life, and the best part is he doesn't ask me any questions concerning what is going on with me. He is just there for me.

I know I can tell him anything about my other side and he is still there in my corner not asking questions just giving me what I need. So at this moment when my depression is weighing on my back like a monkey hanging from a weak tree. Praying that my parents made the right decision about leaving last week. Never thought I would miss them this much. I want to be where he is at, not here in the woods watching my sister show off.

"How long are we going to be out here?" I asked her while she is standing in the middle of this clearing looking like a strained peacock.

"I don't know Ros is there somewhere else you would rather be? And not here assisting your sister?"

192

"To tell you the truth, yes I ... I could be with Jordan right now doing just about anything then standing in the middle of this field watching you."

"How about dying?" We both turned to see a man we have never seen standing on the edge of the woods. "I called a sibling meeting so we could discuss rather or not we were going to sit around and wait until you things destroy us or are we going to do something about it before it's too late. And since I'm here in front of you then you know which way we voted. One thing that you can take with you to the afterlife is you did have a good twenty years."

Before I knew what was happening Rosie had thrown him across the clearing. However, she didn't do it good enough not to put him in the path back towards the school. So we had to run deeper into the woods.

Mom, we're in the woods in the back of the school being chased by a man, I think he might be with another group because he has come to kill us, we are going to run in a circle so we can land back into the clearing to get back to the school. Can you please call the guys to meet us in the clearing behind the football field. Augustas must be in class he's not responding and like idiots, we left our cell phones charging in the room.

Rosalyn we're close, we were just coming to surprise you girls. I can be in the woods in ten minutes, I need for you girls to run around for a few more minutes then head to the clearing where I'll meet up with you.

Running through the woods midday is hard enough, doing it when someone is throwing fireballs at you is just darn near impossible. Rosie is doing her best to throw him off target but it's hard when you are ducking and running and just throwing your hand back hoping you hit your target.

193

Also, I was coming to the realization that I needed to get back into my running, and if we survive this that is exactly what I'm going to do.

Ros, I think it's been enough time, we need to circle back and meet up with mom. About time, I didn't know how long I could last here running like a chicken with no head.

When we entered the clearing we did not see our mom, and I was totally blaming Rosie for this, we should have stayed in the woods longer. I can't believe I'm going to be blown to pieces before I even had the time to become a full woman. I can't go another step I'm dead on my feet. So I do the dumbest thing ever I stop. I have my hands on my knees bent over trying my best to catch my breath.

"Rosalyn, what are you doing, keep going?" My sister screams at me as she passes me.

"I can't, I'm tired Rosie, I just can't. I'm exhausted, beyond the point of passing out. You keep going and come back with mom, I'll keep him busy dodging his fireballs."

"No, I'm not leaving you to face him alone. We are family and family always stick together."

At that moment he came walking out the woods as if he didn't have a care in the world. How smug he is to think we are just some girls, some easy prey that he can do to what he pleases. Okay, maybe the fact that he is a full Fae is the reason he can treat us as easy prey, I just don't like it. I wish I had some powers that I can use to assist. Right now at this moment, I'm so happy that my sister has hers. Without any hesitation, as soon as he came out of the woods he went flying right back in.

"Rosalyn, I need you to give me just a little more energy and run to the school with me before he comes back." I was just about to agree but before he could make it back out our savior showed up. "Mom."

"Where is this man that has been chasing you two?"

"Rosie threw him in the woods, give it a minute he should be coming back out. He's full Fae mom unless he is a witch because he is throwing fireballs like no one's business."

"Get behind me girls. We are going to end this tonight he doesn't survive to come back another day."

At that moment our mother looked up when she heard a noise coming from the trees. "Girls! This is my idiotic brother Gil. I should have guessed it was someone from the family when they said fireballs. You have been wanting this for thirty years, I guess it's a good a time as any for me to teach you a lesson about what a mother would do to protect her children."

"Your children are an abomination that you should have drowned at birth, but no worries after I get done with you I'll kindly do it for you."

That was all my mother needed to hear, she threw a fireball at him so fast it looked like a pitcher throwing an eighty-mile bullet down the lane. It hit him right in the chest, however, it was like nothing had hit him he rocked back and unleashed one of his own.

Our Mom dodged it while throwing one of her own at the same time, he must expect it since he started to lean away, what he didn't expect was the tree limb that Rosie sent his way, to smack him in the face at the same moment. When he went down she proceeded to wrap him in a bunch of vines, but not fast enough, he threw his hand out and threw our mom maybe ten feet.

195

Before she could recover he was up. "Now that she is dealt with I can do what I came to do. Who's first to die?"

He raised his hand and at that moment a blast rang out and he went down in a heap of screaming mess. Rosie and I looked around when my father stepped out of the woods holding his gun. "They have more than one parent, I shot you in your leg, make the wrong move and your head are next, make no mistake about my qualms to kill you over my family. Girls go make sure your mom is alright."

Before we moved she came limping out the woods, "I'll be fine, just a little banged up, you know how sturdy we are."

"Rosie if you could finish what you started. This time does his entire body." She raised her hands and wrapped several vines tightly around him, from his chest to his ankles, tight enough where he couldn't move. He was however cursing me and my sister. While lying there with a bullet wound in his leg.

"Rosalyn. I know you would rather do anything else in the world but do what I am about to ask you to do. But will you please heal his leg so he is not bleeding everywhere?"

I went to touch his leg to heal him and he began trying to roll away from me. "I'll rather die than have that abomination touch me. Don't you put your hands on me, little girl."

"Don't tempt me, Gil. I'll leave you here for the wildlife if you don't shut up. Matter of fact honey will you put something in his mouth."

"Gladly," replied my dad. And that was the last time we heard him speak another word. I looked at my Mom with a new sense of pride and love. Who else would be thinking about healing someone that came to kill her children, but my mother. "Mom, what are you going to do with him?"

196

"I'm shipping him back to Azurion with a note telling them that the next time they send someone to harm someone in my family, they will be returning in a body bag. That way they know not to try this again."

I have never been a girl that liked to cry, but at that moment the tears wouldn't stop coming, I hugged my Mom and cried, I cried for the life that she gave me, I cried for the life that I took for granted, and I cried for the life that she continued to grace me with by protecting me tonight. As only a mother could it was if she knew because she did not say anything she just rocked me back and forth.

If not for Rosie's sweet little gift we would have had a long time getting Gil out of the area. Using her Telekinesis she was able to levitate him out the woods, and I was glad for it since we couldn't go through past the football field, we had to travel through the woods in the opposite direction of the school until we got to our parent's car. It took us about thirty minutes to get there but we made it.

After putting Gil in the trunk of the car. Our mom told us to go back to school and let her handle it. Instead of coming up for just a weekend, our parents ended up staying for an entire week, we spent so much of our free time with them, that Sapphire, Rosie, and I were on the verge of booking them a cruise until graduation.

There is only so much parent mode you can take when you want to have a romantic dinner/movie night with your guy. I never asked mom what happened with her brother, I actually didn't care. I just didn't want anyone else coming after me or my sister. Jordan wondered why my parents were sticking around so long. I couldn't keep the dangers from him any longer. When he picked me up that night I filled him in.

"Remember the night you called Rosie and I was hanging out in the clearing behind the football field? I told you that Rosie was out there practicing and wouldn't want an audience?"

"Yeah, what about it?"

"While we were there a man showed up that we had never met before, he was there to kill us because according to him and my Mom's family we are an abomination, so he was doing us justice. We had been chased and darn near killed by I guess I would have to say our uncle or my mother's brother. My Mom and Dad showed up right on time and kicked his butt and sent him packing back to where he came from. I told you to let you know what you're going to be up against being in a relationship with me."

"What would that be my love, kicking some butt and ignoring the names? You are my heart, my love, and my life. Your fight is my fight, my survival depends on your survival. So, you telling me about your extended family does not scare me off, it pisses me off and I pity any of them that I meet attempting to do something to you, and Rosie as an extension of you. I just hate that we don't have the same link as Rosie and Augustas so you could have called me. I don't like that I wasn't there to help defend you."

I grabbed his face and gave him a quick smack on the lips. "Next time."

"As much as I would love to defend your honor. I hope there is no next time."

⊕

Go figure I would be possibly coming down with something. Fae doesn't usually get sick, but since it took so long for me to get my powers, I think the human side of me is just as active as the Fae side.

Today is a bad day, I don't feel well. Ironic a person with healing powers unable to heal herself. Fae isn't supposed to get sick, but Fae isn't supposed to take four years for their special power to manifest.

I'm glad my senior year is my easiest year, I'm pretty much done with classes I just have to finish my rotation at the clinic and get my evaluation from them, complete my final essay, and turn that in and relax in my spare time. I just need to stay busy so it doesn't catch up with me, whatever it may be.

So to keep my mind busy so I wouldn't change it and go looking for Jordan and whine about how I feel. I decide to volunteer at the adult living facility. It gave me a sense of purpose of being useful to the elderly whenever they became ill, I would slowly heal them.

Sometimes I wished I could do it faster but miraculous healing is the last thing I need to be associated with only the times I am there, and someone putting two and two together. So slow and steady is the way that I go. My mornings are spent doing my rotations and my nights are spent at home.

That made sure I had little time for anything else, no parties, no socializing. I can't remember the last time I went to the movies or hung out at the diner with the crew. I guess this was just getting me ready for what life was going to be like when I graduate in a month's time. Any free time I had was spent with Jordan.

# CHAPTER 20

The day of graduation did not start the way I thought it would be. I need to get out of this room, I feel as if I'm burning up inside, something is seriously wrong. I think I need to release some energy.

"Hey, Ro, I'm going to go for a run." There's no answer, I look at my watch it's early I wonder where she's at? I'll just write her a note, so she won't miss me and leave without me when she gets back.

At that moment Theresa comes walking into the common area. "Did I hear you say you're going for a run? Did you want me to come with?"

"Naw, it's cool, I'm just going to run-up to the Quad, around the pond and back, thirty minutes tops." She bobs her head turns on her heels and goes back into her room. I wasn't trying to be rude, but I have a lot on my mind. What that guy Gil said about us and the prophecy has been on my mind heavy.

I have plans for my future and they do not include giving them up trying to stay safe from some whacked out Fae. For now, I'm just going to go on this run to relieve some of this stress. I feel as if something wonky is going on with my powers. I know I shouldn't be feeling this bad. If after this run I feel the same way I will call my Mom and ask her about it.

Turning the corner I see something in the middle of the Pond. What is that? Is that, no it can't be, she is not due back for another two hours still. Now my eyes are playing tricks on me. I really must not be feeling well, as I was passing an opening, I could have sworn I saw something that cannot be real. Maybe what I needed was more sleep. This fever or whatever it is messing with my head. I'll finish my run to the Pond and head back.

What the Fizznic. Coming in full view of the pond I see that my eyes were correct in what they were seeing. Why is Danielle walking on the half-frozen pond? Doesn't she know how dangerous that is to her safety and mine if I have to rescue her?

"Danielle, D, Hey, DANIELLE!!!!" Why in the world is she not responding? I run towards her continuing to call her name with no reply. Wait a dang on minute. What is that sound? Please tell me the ice is not cracking under her feet. She's still standing there so it can't be.

When I get closer the sound gets louder. I see that-, NO! that is definitely the sound of ice breaking. "DANIELLELLL! RUN!" Come on why is she not moving, what is going on. She fell. Looking around I don't see anyone out here. what am I going to do?

I run across the field. I have to get her out before it's too late. What was she doing out here anyway? Why was she standing on the ice? Why didn't she respond when I was screaming her name. Wondering to myself won't get her out of this ice. Lying here looking at my bestfriend float away is the worst feeling ever. Not being the right twin to save her is worst.

Please, fairy father of stars, mother of earth, show me what to do to save a part of my heart. I close my eyes and all I can do is picture what I wish I had the ability to do. I picture being able to drag her body back towards the hole and lifting her out of the water, I picture me laying her down beside me and everything being alright.

But deep in my heart I know when I open my eyes my bestfriend will still be in the water. Ro, I have to call Ro, maybe she will get here in time to guide her out for me to heal her. She's not answering. Why isn't she answering? I know she had to run into town this morning but why is she not answering my call?

I close my eyes again. I can't see my friend die like this. With all that is in me, I wish that I was able to bring her back, that I had the power the Rosie does, that I was worthy enough to be able to save my friend.

When I open my eyes to grab my phone to call one of the guys, I get the shock of my life, there is Danielle right there lying beside me. But how? I look around for just a moment to see if I see anyone. I don't and I don't care, right now my focus has to be on Danielle.

I don't hesitate. I try to heal her but what I'm doing is not enough, she's not waking up. "Danielle, please wake up." "Danielle, do you hear me? Wake up...Why were you here?" With my hand still on her pouring all the healing power I can into her. I call the ambulance and I call my twin, the last thing on this earth I want to do is lose my bestfriend. She's still not answering my call.

"Come on Rosie pick up. Pick up, pick up." She doesn't answer so I call Theresa. She picks up on the third ring. "Theresa, drive over here by the pond on the other side of the Quad,"

"Um, why would I do that? Do you not know what time it is?" "Danielle is hurt."

"What do you mean she's hurt?"

"Like I said she's hurt, she isn't waking up. I called the ambulance and they're on the way, but I don't want to leave her to get the car."

"What happened?"

"I don't know, I can only tell you what I saw, and I'll gladly do that once you get here." I know Theresa isn't trying to annoy me but her constant questioning and not moving are doing just that.

"I'm pulling up now, I was moving while we were talking."

Theresa rushes over and drops down near Danielle shaking her softly trying to get her to open her eyes.

"Did you try to heal her?"

"Yes, of course, she was not breathing at first, I was able to get her breathing, but I can't get her to wake up. I called the ambulance, they on the way. I also called Rosie she's not answering. Have you heard from her?"

"No, not since she left this morning to go and work on her senior project."

There are several questions that I ask myself. What was she doing out here anyway? Why is she back so soon? Matter of fact, where is her car? I didn't see it on my run. How did she even get here? As Danielle is being taken away in the ambulance all I can wonder is if this is the last summer I'll spend with her. We have been friends forever and I cannot imagine life without her in it.

We follow the ambulance to the hospital. Waiting to hear is the worst. I called Danielle's parents, and I call the guys. Augustas tells me that he was about to call me. Rosie was in an accident on her way back from town and she is in the emergency room right now being looked at. After he tells me that she called out to him through their link when the accident happened.

I feel bad for shutting ours down so I could focus on my end of senior year activities. I'm so grateful my sister can speak to Augustas in her head, we would have never known what happened to her.  And I would be possibly losing two people right now.

Today is our graduation day, we're supposed to be receiving our certificates of completion in the next few hours.  Not sitting in a hospital awaiting news. My parents came rushing in a little after

I got there. Augustas must have called them. I didn't even think about them, my mind was so focused on Danielle.

Not soon after my parents show up do her parents show up. Sitting here waiting on word on my twin and my bestfriend is the hardest thing I have ever had to do in my life, I can't help but imagine how quickly life can turn on you.

When everything gets torn apart that's when you finally start to realize what matters. I thought that if I just ignored my lack of power everything would just fall into place. I would be safe, and things would go back to being normal again. But is anything in life normal, or safe, or even simple.

It's not just some game divided into heroes and villains, supernatural and human, good versus evil. Life is just people trying to make the best of what they are given. That is what I need to start doing. After this is all said and done, I will make sure to enjoy my sister and bestfriend to the fullest.

We're all here now and sitting around waiting to hear from the doctors about the condition of two of the most important people in all our lives. After I tell everyone what I observed at the school, and Augustas tells them the little he observed about Rosie.

Danielle's parents and my parents are in a deep discussion about what they are going to do about our safety when this is all over. It's kind of hard to discuss really openly anything with them since they don't know what we are.

We downplayed Rosie's accident, and of course, we had no idea why Danielle was even on the pond in the first place since she was nonresponsive when we got here. I heard my mother saying something about, maybe putting off anyone going or doing anything in the near future until all of this is settled. I was about to interrupt with my own two cents when everything came to a halt.

"We were wrong, and we need your help." I look up to see eight individuals standing in front of me.

"Who are you? Mom. Who are these people?"

"They're the heads of each individual sector from my hometown."

"What are you doing here?" Asked my mother, walking out of earshot of everyone and taking them into the hall outside the waiting room. My Dad and I followed along. When we got out there we just turned, awaiting a reply to the burning question of their appearance now of all the times to come.

"Your girls are not a curse. They're our saviors."

Will Rosie and Rosalyn do what is expected of them?
Next in the series   The Cursed Fae (Secrets, Lies, & Betrayal Book 3)

# ACKNOWLEDGMENTS

First and foremost I would like to thank my Heavenly Father for giving me the words to put on the paper. Blessing me with the ideas and the know-how to get this series written.

I would like to give a special thanks to my family and most importantly to my readers. I am extremely grateful for the ones that read this book my Mother Lucille Green and my Son Anthony who gave some insight that allowed me the opportunity to be able to share with the rest of the world. A special thanks to my son's Antwaun and Andrik whose belief in me and my vision helped me to push through the fog.

My stories are full of magic, mayhem, self-awareness, and mystery. I create havoc that will have the reader deeply involved in these pursuits. I have always been interested in paranormal stories that involve all kinds of creatures and beings.

I could never find a story about the Fae that didn't show them in a negative light. With great love and passion, I put pen to paper, and my first book The Cursed Fae Series was born.

I also need to recognize Mrs Ann Bey of SMAC Talk. Thank you for your guidance, assistance, and encouraging words. If not for you many times I would have been lost in the sea of self-publishing. Best life-coach ever.

https://www.mrsannbey.com/

Also, thank you L-V-Productions for editing my book and creating my cover page. Having you do the heavy lifting allowed me to work on my craft of just writing the story. I loved what you did with book 1 The Power That Destroys and I love what you have done with this book also. I can't wait to see what you come up with for book 3 Secrets, Lies, and Betrayal.

l-v-productions